Wu Dang
fist of the wanderer

AIRSHIP 27 PRODUCTIONS

Wu Dang: Fist of the Wanderer
© 2018 Barbara Doran

Published by Airship 27 Productions
www.airship27.com
www.airship27hangar.com

Interior illustrations © 2018 Gary Kato
Cover illustration © 2018 Rob Davis

Editor: Ron Fortier
Associate Editor: Jaime Ramos
Marketing and Promotions Manager: Michael Vance
Production and design by Rob Davis.

ISBN-13: 978-1-946183-39-2
ISBN-10: 1-946183-39-3

Printed in the United States of America

10 9 8 7 6 5 4 3 2 1

Wu Dang
fist of the wanderer

By Barbara Doran

Chapter 1: Metal — Obedience Leads to Great Power

The Chinese were fighting again.

Captain Jake Burton was accustomed to Shanghai's constant noise; drunken sailors going to and fro, street vendors hawking their wares, horses and mules clopping through the streets, dragging carts and carriages. The street fights, on the other hand, were a new and disconcerting development. They were also a dangerous one for any foreigner fool enough to wander onto the battlefield.

The trouble found Burton in Old Town, the part of Shanghai reserved for native Chinese and a place he usually avoided. Americans—especially six foot tall Americans with light brown hair and blue eyes—stood out like a sore thumb here. He was conscious of being the center of attention, though no one was rude enough to stare outright. "Trouble with you, Jake, is you're too greedy," he muttered to himself.

Still, Burton's would-be client was obviously rich. The courier who'd brought the invitation had been dressed in fine dark blue silk, his carefully shaved forehead polished to near mirror smoothness. Everything about him had suggested wealth and importance. Whoever Lang He Xiao was, he was obviously a member of China's ruling class. No Manchu courier would work for a Han, no matter how rich and influential.

Burton was nearing his destination when a howl of rage came from a nearby alley, followed by the sound of shattering wood. Knowing better than to hang around when someone started shouting slogans and breaking things, he turned down another alley. He chose poorly, walking straight into a small gang of men in grey trousers, their lean torsos bared to reveal tattoos of butterflies, each carrying heavy cleavers.

"I don't suppose any of you speak English?" Burton asked, backing up. He understood Chinese, could even speak it—badly—but this wasn't the time for comic translation errors.

Someone shouted angrily behind Burton and he didn't need to look to know he was pinned between the first gang and another so similarly dressed the only way to tell the difference were their headbands; the words Heaven's Fist written on them in Chinese. Both gangs were Han, with the characteristic queue required by Qing law.

Burton was an experienced sailor and he wasn't afraid of a few cuts and bruises. He did draw the line at being outnumbered. Besides, it was obvious he wasn't their target. He searched for an escape route, while the two groups shouted at each other. Threats, mostly, with descriptions of ancestors and mating habits that didn't need translation.

The fight began when one of the Heaven's Fist gang shoved one of the Butterflies, knocking him to the ground. Immediately, the others jostled for position, swinging their blades and yelling incoherently. Blood spurted and men shrieked as each side did their best to slice the other. Disinclined to be fileted with the rest, Burton pressed back against the wall and struggled to get past. He could see the main road—and safety—mere feet away. All he had to do was reach it.

Something tugged Burton's trouser leg. A quick glance downward showed him a young man peeking out through a narrow crack in the wall. The youth beckoned quickly, adding, "Come," in Chinese. It wouldn't be easy to follow, Burton being bigger and heavier than his would-be rescuer. It was also his best chance.

Forcing his way down to join the stranger, Burton followed the youngster through the wall. As he'd feared, it was tight, but the bricks crumbled as he pushed, slowly giving way and letting him through into a badly rundown courtyard.

The young man pulled Burton to his feet with easy and surprising strength. He was skinny and short—barely coming to Burton's shoulder—but his grip was rock hard. Before Burton could say a word of thanks, his rescuer turned and headed for the open doorway of an old Chinese house. Once again he called, "Come."

"Hey. Wait. Who are you?"

The youth didn't answer, leaving Burton to decide whether he should cooperate. With some rare exceptions, Westerners weren't welcome in Chinese homes. Moreover, the young man was the oddest Chinese Burton had ever encountered. Roughly dressed in patched trousers and an equally patched short robe, his general appearance was at odds with what Burton had become accustomed to.

He'd seen the queues Han Chinese wore. He'd seen the carefully shaven foreheads of the Manchus. He'd even seen utterly bald Buddhist monks. But this man's unshaven black hair fell to his waist, as straight and silky as a young girl's. Indeed, Burton might have mistaken him for a woman if not for his dry tenor. Well, that, and most women didn't have such strong features.

Ordinarily, Burton would have taken his own risks and headed else-where. This time he couldn't. There wasn't anywhere to go and the young man had come to his aid in a time of need. Distrustfully, aware of being out of his depth, Burton trailed behind the youth, letting him lead the way inside.

ooo

Yi Xiao hurried through Old Man Fang's mansion, hoping to reach the front door before anyone noticed him. Or, rather, before anyone noticed his giant-sized companion. Alone, he could have escaped easily. With Burton along, his chances dropped significantly. Especially since the man would not stop talking.

Behind Yi Xiao, Burton commented on the furnishings. "A little bit tatty, that hanging, but it'd fetch a pretty penny back in New York." His voice was rumbling thunder and sure to attract attention. Or would if the latest battle between the Heavenly Fist Society and their long term rivals, the Butterfly Blades, weren't more interesting.

"And my sister is quite fond of the porcelain dishes. Though the last set I brought back for her shattered on the way home."

Yi Xiao stopped and glared at his companion, making the silencing gesture he'd learned from his father's second wife. "Will you please be quiet?"

A startled expression crossed Burton's face. "You speak English? Perfect British English?"

"Not now!" Yi Xiao snapped. "We have to get out of here. Master says, save your breath for when it's needed."

"I don't even know where here is! Or who this master is you're talking about...." Burton trailed off. "Wait. This isn't your home?"

Yi Xiao sighed, indicating his ragged clothes. "Do I look like I belong to a rich merchant's family?"

"How'd you get in then? Are you a thief?"

"I climbed the wall and no. Will you come?"

"I don't know. I might be better off throwing myself on the mercy of... whomever it is that lives here. Who does live here, by the way?" Burton eyed the furnishings. "And are you sure they're rich? This place looks a bit run down."

"Pawn Merchants like Old Man Fang don't waste their money on frip-peries," Yi Xiao retorted. "Bodyguards, on the other hand...." He gestured sharply behind Burton as two big, overly armed and armored men approached. In Chinese, he added, "So sorry to have disturbed. We were just passing through."

The attempt to ease the bodyguards' minds had exactly the effect Yi Xiao expected. Which was to say, none at all. He grabbed Burton's wrist and dragged him towards the front of the building. "Run!"

Burton might be irritating and incapable of doing anything without running off at the mouth but he knew where he wasn't wanted. "If you aren't a thief," he grumbled, following behind Yi Xiao, "Why are you here?"

Yi Xiao ducked past a third bodyguard, just coming around the corner as his fellows shouted for help. "To get you out of that mess, Captain Burton."

Naming the foreigner was a mistake. Burton stopped in his tracks, nearly dragging Yi Xiao off his feet. "You know who I am? Were you following me?"

"Yes, I know. Yes, I was." Before Burton could demand more, Yi Xiao dodged behind him, catching hold of the nearest bodyguard's wrist and redirecting the man's attack before he could grasp hold of Burton's collar. Flinging the bodyguard against the wall he drew on his inner strength and thrust the base of his palm into the man's side. Padded armor, strong enough to take most blows, proved useless. A rib snapped in a most satisfying way beneath Yi Xiao's blow.

The bodyguard growled a curse and slammed Yi Xiao backwards, or tried to. Giving way to the blow, Yi Xiao slid sideways and under the man's arm. At the same time he hooked the man's knee and dropped him to the ground.

Unexpectedly, Burton sided with Fang's bodyguards, striking Yi Xiao from behind with something hard and heavy. Unprepared for the attack and focused on the other men, Yi Xiao went down, only dimly aware of Burton saying, "Now gentlemen, that proves he isn't with me. I don't suppose you'd let me go?"

The sound of a bodyguard's fist hitting Burton's jaw was oddly satisfying.

○○○

When Burton came to, he and his erstwhile rescuer had been tied up and stuck in a cellar. At least, he assumed the other person in the musty darkness was his erstwhile rescuer. Someone was breathing a short distance away from Burton, shallow ragged breaths like a sailor coming off a bender.

"I expect an apology, you realize?" the young man said suddenly.

"Why should I? I get caught in a fight and you conveniently show up to drag me through some rich sod's house to get caught by his bodyguards? You know who I am when we've never even met? What am I supposed to think?"

The fellow went silent. Then he asked in a puzzled way, "Sod? Why would you call Old Man Fang a lump of dirt?"

For the first time Burton realized the limitations of his companion's English. His near perfect British accent had fooled Burton into talking to him like a native speaker. "It's slang. For sodomite."

"I... see." The young man paused, then said in a defeated way. "No. I don't see. What is a sodomite?"

Now Burton was embarrassed and he decided to end the conversation. "Ask your tutor. I'm not here to give you English lessons." He took a deep breath and fell to coughing at the stench of something old, moldy and somewhat sulfurous. "Never mind. How do you know who I am? And who are you, anyway?"

"I know who you are because I was sent to make sure you arrived safely, Captain Burton. As for who I am; I am called the Wanderer, my surname is Lang, my personal name is Yi Xiao, and I am the youngest and least worthy grandson of Lang He Xiao. Along with being your guide in this nonsensical adventure, I am but a humble would-be priest of no particular note."

If it hadn't been entirely too dark to do so, Burton would have glared at his companion. "You? A priest? With all that hair?" He was certain the fellow wasn't Christian. Nothing about him suggested such a thing.

"You're thinking of Buddhist priests. I am, or try to be, a follower of the *Dao*." By now Yi Xiao was beside Burton, undoing the ropes binding him. "Not successfully, I admit, or you wouldn't have been able to strike me, earlier."

Burton didn't waste time scoffing. "So you were protecting me? Why?"

"Because a *guilao* in Old Town sticks out like a pine in a rice field."

It took Burton a moment to remember what *guilao* meant. 'Ghost' or 'Foreigner'. The word many Chinese used for Westerners. "Well, yes, I suppose that's true. But if your boss didn't want me to stick out, maybe he should have met me elsewhere." There were plenty of places in Shanghai where people could meet privately.

"My... boss... is elderly and doesn't care for the foreign districts of Shanghai." Yi Xiao sighed. "In any event, all this is getting us nowhere. Old Fang has sent for the city guards and I'd rather not attract their attention." Cloth rustled as he rose to his feet.

"How do we get out of here?"

"Fortunately, this is a storage cellar beneath Old Fang's kitchen. They've probably set a guard but I can deal with one or two men. Given, of course, no one knocks me unconscious from behind."

Burton refused to be embarrassed. No one had told him to expect a guard after all. As Yi Xiao moved around the room, searching for the exit, Burton asked, "What about that fight? Was it what you were protecting me from?"

"It's over and yes. Not because you were their target. Things are a trifle up in the air these days. The Daoguang Emperor's illness has set China reeling. Every triad, every society, every citizen of the rivers and lakes are vying for dominance." Yi Xiao shifted again, adding, "Now be quiet a moment, if you can. I'm not good enough to do this while distracted. Master says, silence is worth its weight in gold."

Burton was just about to complain that he could, so, be quiet when it occurred to him that he'd be proving the opposite. He waited, listening to Yi Xiao's breathing, puzzled by its slow cadence. What was the man doing? And why did he feel like he could see Yi Xiao's outline in the darkness ahead of him? He'd just decided there must be some faint light after all when the man let loose a sharp cry.

Wood smashed above them and light flared. Somewhere in the distance a man shouted angrily. Burton didn't need Yi Xiao's urging to run for it.

ooo

With the fight outside Old Man Fang's mansion over, Yi Xiao thought it safe to leave by the back gate, rather than attempt the house again. This, however, meant explaining himself to Burton, who had a regrettable tendency to demand answers without thinking for himself. "I was hoping to use the distraction of the fight to escape through the front. I didn't know you have more words than a pond has carp."

The insult set Burton's jaw going twice as fast as it had before. Yi Xiao was a rude bastard, a brat with no consideration for a lost foreigner, an arrogant boy who didn't know how to treat his betters. Being busy watching for trouble, Yi Xiao ignored the nervous babblings of a frightened man.

When trouble came, it came from an unexpected source. Yi Xiao was watching for someone to take offense to his charge's presence. Instead, he found himself face to face with an angry stranger, this one heavy-set, wild-haired and clearly looking for a fight. From his accent, he was Taiwanese. From his clothes, he was a dockworker searching for adventure. From his expression, Yi Xiao was the adventure he searched for.

"You!" the man shouted, waving his fist within inches of Yi Xiao's nose. "I know you!"

"My dear sir, I'm afraid I don't know you at all." Yi Xiao tried to nudge Burton off to the side. The man didn't cooperate. "Where is it you think we've met?"

Another swipe, this one close enough to set Yi Xiao's hair fluttering. "Don't play the fool with me, you damn Manchu bastard! You stole my woman at Golden Phoenix in Soochow four months ago!"

Yi Xiao couldn't help being side-tracked. "The Golden Phoenix? However did you manage to get in? You don't look like you can afford their prices. Besides, whomever you met, it wasn't me. I've been training on Heng Shan for the last two years."

"Weren't you just telling me not to judge a person by their possessions?" Burton commented. "And shouldn't you mention you weren't there before quibbling over details?"

"Possibly." Yi Xiao noted the American understood Chinese. He'd have to warn his grandmother. "I tend to forget myself sometimes."

"Given he's ready to break that long nose of yours, you might not want to do that."

Yi Xiao returned his attention to his would-be attacker. "May I suggest the French Quarter? I'm sure a fine gentleman like yourself can find plenty of willing companions there. Cheaper, too."

The man growled, about to swing his fist again, but Yi Xiao raised a hand, "One moment. I have a rule about fighting."

"Yeah, he's a priest, you know. You don't expect a man of God to know how to fight."

Yi Xiao ignored Burton's base canard, asking his would-be opponent, "What's your name?"

"Feng. Feng Mei Sheng!"

The man wasn't familiar. If he was part of the martial world—and Yi Xiao doubted it—he wasn't important. More likely he was a street tough looking for a reason to fight. "Very well, Mei Sheng, I charge a hundred *tael* for every blow you land."

Both Mei Sheng and Burton stared at him. "What?!"

"You're a strong fellow and medicine's expensive," Yi Xiao pointed out. "If you hit me, I'll be needing to see a doctor."

Infuriated, Mei Sheng took a step forward and struck hard. Yi Xiao twisted sideways, just as the man's fist brushed his shoulder. "Of course, you do have to hit me first. I won't charge if you miss. That wouldn't be fair."

Now Mei Sheng was utterly furious, slamming his fists into Yi Xiao as hard as he could. Or, rather, slamming his fists into thin air. Yi Xiao was not yet a true master, but a poorly trained and foul-tempered streetfighter would need luck or carefully hidden skill to get a blow past his evasions.

Mei Sheng had both. His next flurry of attacks drew Yi Xiao's attention in the wrong direction, giving the man an opening. He took it without hesitation, his kick strong and high. Stocky though he was, the man's reach was unexpected and disconcerting. Yi Xiao was sent flying, landing in the dirt and rolling backwards to his feet. Someone in the gathering crowd yelled an insult; he'd lost a bet thanks to Yi Xiao's inattention.

"Master says, don't get cocky," Yi Xiao reminded himself ruefully. Then he was dodging his attacker again, paying attention to the man's lower body. He ought to have known better than to ignore it before. Even the least experienced fighter's attacks could be read in the movement of their feet and hips.

This time he spotted the shift in weight heralding another kick. This time he twisted out of its way. This time he caught hold of Mei Sheng's leg and lifted it higher, dropping its owner onto his back. The man slammed into the dirt, to the great amusement of their growing audience.

"You dirty bastard! You rotten little pig-swiver!" The flow of invective was educational, but Yi Xiao already knew most of it. He dropped one knee into the man's throat, controlling the urge to shatter his windpipe. Unaware of how close he'd come to death, the man howled, "Get off me!"

"No. Listen to me carefully. This foolishness is going to get attention. The city guards are busy cleaning up another fight, but once they have, they'll be headed here." Yi Xiao tapped the man's nose lightly. "Now, who sent you to attack me?"

A startled look filled Mei Sheng's eyes. "How'd you... I mean, no one!"

"That's a lie. You're a better fighter than you look. More importantly, I doubt any dockworker would hold a grudge over one of Mrs. Song's girls. Not for four months. So who hired you?" Yi Xiao pressed his knee a little harder against the man's sternum to keep his attention.

Wilting, Mei Sheng admitted, "I didn't get his name. But he said you took the girl he was going to buy."

The whole thing made no sense. Yi Xiao had never been in the Golden Phoenix, though his brother, horrible gossip that Yi De was, had mentioned the place in his letters. Not that his staid elder brother ever went there. It was their cousin, ever given to slipping off and evading his keepers, who liked the place. With a sense of inevitability, Yi Xiao asked, "How'd you know it was me?"

The man reached up and Yi Xiao caught his hand quickly. "In my pocket," Mei Sheng protested. "A drawing. I've been following your trail all around the country."

Yi Xiao found a tattered sheet of paper with a face painted on it. Mirror familiar features gazed back at him; long face, thin straight nose, narrow lips. The only real difference was the hairstyle. He grasped hold of his long forelocks. "Do you think this is four months growth?" Most Manchu men shaved the front of their heads, keeping only enough hair for their braids. Yi Xiao, as a priest of the *Dao*, hadn't had a razor near his scalp for two years now.

Mei Sheng looked embarrassed. "I... er.... well...."

Standing up and pulling the man to his feet, Yi Xiao said, "I hold no grudge. Here." He put a hundred *tael* coin into his erstwhile opponent's hand. "Go find yourself a doctor."

"Wait. Why?"

"I'm a priest, not a street fighter." Admittedly and embarrassingly, Yi Xiao had enjoyed himself rather too much. But that didn't change the fact that a seeker of the *Dao* shouldn't be brawling in the street like a common thug. He hesitated, torn between secrets he could not reveal and the knowledge that this man's quest would get him killed. "Take the money and some advice. Drop this matter. Repay your benefactor if you have to but don't keep hunting for the man in this painting. You won't survive."

Mei Sheng snorted. "Why? Is he that good? Better than you?"

"No. Quite the opposite." Yi Xiao handed the picture back. "But he's too well protected. If you did get to him, you'd never escape the consequences. The death of a thousand slices might be the least of your worries. Even I dare not raise a hand to him."

It took Mei Sheng a moment to understand. He folded the paper up carefully and said, "We'll see. You may be right after all."

As Mei Sheng turned and walked away, Yi Xiao returned his attention to his companion, who'd been watching the fight with a mix of confusion and amusement. In English, he added, "Come along, Burton. You have an appointment and it's high time you got to it."

○○○

Burton couldn't help being annoyed. Accustomed to command, he didn't like being dragged around like a toddler. Admittedly the most recent fight had been Yi Xiao's own problem but he'd felt a fifth wheel, waiting for the pair to finish their argument. He was also glad not to have to fight Yi Xiao himself. There'd been a moment when it'd looked like the man would kill his attacker.

"That picture did look like you," he commented as Yi Xiao led him towards a large round entranceway through a white wall. A shorter wall blocked their path inside, forcing them to go around it; another example of Chinese evasiveness and circuitous thinking.

"It wasn't."

They entered a large courtyard where a dozen Manchurian men were doing their afternoon exercises. Burton had seen this sort of thing before, visiting his Chinese contacts in the business district. Apparently it both kept the servants fit and too tired to get into trouble.

"A relative?" Burton pressed, sensing weakness and finding it irresistible. He ignored the fists and staffs striking through the air, though some came within half a foot of him as they passed. "Your twin brother, maybe?"

"I don't have a twin." An elderly servant greeted Yi Xiao and at a word from the young man, went back inside. "We need to clean up. I've sent for someone to take you to your room."

Burton hadn't intended to stay but he didn't get a chance to argue. Yi Xiao headed off in another direction and two pretty young maids came out to persuade Burton into slippers and lead him into the house. Deciding not to argue, he let the pair take him to an attractive little room with a bowl for washing his hands and a plain blue silk robe for him to put on over his clothes.

"Please will you change?" one of the girls asked, bowing. "The Elder should be respected."

Cleaning up only took a few minutes. The robe covered the worst of Burton's sins and the rest, his hands and face, weren't so dirty as to be noticeable. All he had to do was scrub them quickly and make sure his fingernails were clean. As for his hair, it was generally a tousled mess no comb had ever tamed. He doubted anything could be done about it this late in the day.

Once Burton dressed he stepped out and looked around. Now this was the sort of place he expected a rich merchant to own. The halls were ivory tinted plaster. The ceiling was covered in elaborately carved tiles. The floor was fine and well-varnished wood. More tellingly, there were paintings and other *objet d'art* decorating every flat surface, from walls to counter. If he could bring these things back with him to New York he'd be set for life.

"There you are." Yi Xiao had changed to a simple mauve robe. He'd even tied his hair back into a sleek knot at the top of his skull. Accustomed as Burton was to the ubiquitous queue, the hair style was mildly startling. "Come along."

They walked through elegant halls to a small room towards the back of the house, its walls covered in bookshelves. A desk stood across from Burton and he had a queasy flashback to his first ship, his first captain and his first and nearly last mistake. At least this time he wouldn't be blamed for having forced his fellow crewmembers to cut a necessary rope before it could drag him straight into the deep.

There was a thin, elderly, woman sitting at the desk, dressed in padded dark silk embroidered with chrysanthemums. Her hair was completely grey and her eyes were slightly clouded, but she had a look that made Burton think she must have been quite spirited and headstrong when she was younger.

The lady was reading an English newspaper with a dark frown. She muttered under her breath, then slammed the paper down with a cold snort. Tall as he was, it was easy to see what she'd been reading. Something about the Daoguang Emperor's illness. Yi Xiao had said the man was sick and now Burton remembered there was a very young and inexperienced heir waiting in the wings. What was the youngster's name? Oh, yes, that was right. Yi Zhu.

Looking up at her grandson, the woman raised a brow. "Where is your willow leaf knife?" she demanded in Chinese.

"Grandmother," Yi Xiao bowed three times then went to his knees and abased himself against the floor. "I greet you."

"Rise, youngest grandson. Introduce me to the foreigner. Do not bother with my titles. We don't have time for that nonsense."

Yi Xiao obeyed. "Grandmother, this is Captain Jake Burton." In English, he added, "Captain, this is the head of the Lang family, He Xiao. You may refer to her as Madam Lang."

Burton was startled, but he bowed nonetheless, not bothering with the kowtow. He didn't regard it as shameful the way some did, but it also wasn't his style. He wasn't even sure how many he might be expected to offer, especially to someone who—despite not wishing to mention it—was clearly some sort of nobility. A mere merchant wouldn't have titles to omit.

Haltingly, because he understood Chinese better than he spoke it, Burton said, "Pleased meeting you, ma'am." His limit reached, he added in English, "Er... am I right, thinking she's the one who invited me?" Women back home weren't so forward. Hell, women in China usually weren't either. But this lady, lean, elderly and austere, might be a queen or a princess. She wasn't the sort to leave her business to others.

Yi Xiao was about to answer when Madam Lang interrupted. "You distracted me. Where is your willow leaf knife?"

Cheeks bright with embarrassment, Yi Xiao told her, "I'm done with weapons. I left it back at Heng Shan."

Madam Lang's expression might have frozen boiling water. She was so coldly angry Burton knew his presence alone prevented her from telling her grandson what she thought of his decision. Guessing defending the youth wouldn't help, Burton held his tongue.

"Do not think you are safe simply because this foreigner is with you," the old woman stated calmly. "We will discuss your feckless irresponsibility to the rivers and lakes later."

"Yes, Grandmother." Yi Xiao bowed his head, then turned an embarrassed look at Burton. "Private business," he added in English. "No need to worry about it."

"No doubt. I don't suppose you'd like to get to the point now? I am a busy man."

The old woman's English was probably no better than Burton's Chinese but she understood enough. "Assist me," she ordered Yi Xiao. "We must not keep our guest waiting."

Another bow and Yi Xiao moved to stand behind Madam Lang. Once he'd done so, his grandmother began to speak and he to translate. "You are the captain of the *Henrietta Marie*."

"I am. And a fine barque she is, too." Burton had scrimped and saved for her, borrowing heavily from his family back in New York. He was as proud of the little vessel as if she were his own child. "I've already filled her hold, though, so if you're hoping to sell me something...."

"I am not a merchant, Captain Burton. I have nothing to sell you. Rather, I must send a package to San Francisco. It is valuable; one of our family's greatest treasures, but it cannot remain in China. The risk is too great."

Burton frowned. "I'm not going to San Francisco, ma'am. I'm headed to San Diego and south from there to Panama."

With a smile, the old woman inclined her head. "San Diego is sufficient, Captain. The package can find its way to San Francisco on its own."

Yi Xiao stared at his grandmother with a confused expression. He plainly had no idea what the endangered treasure was she wished to send away. The boy obviously knew better than to ask, but he was desperately curious.

For that matter, so was Burton. Packages, especially important and valuable packages, generally didn't travel on their own. "It's rude to inquire, but how exactly do you plan on getting it from San Diego to San Francisco safely?"

"Given he's been walking all over Heng Shan's peaks these past two years, I believe he can find his way unassisted. Can't you, grandson?"

ooo

Yi Xiao prided himself on staying calm through the strangest of circumstances. Yet the news he was being sent to America made him forget his manners. Instead of translating his grandmother's last words, he demanded, "WHAT?" in a voice that broke in a way it hadn't for years.

"Do not stop translating, boy. The Captain is a busy man and we don't want to waste his time." His grandmother's voice was ice and stone and he knew he'd done wrong to question her in front of an outsider.

Another man might have argued. Another man might have walked out on the whole mess. Another man was not the youngest male descendant of the Imperial Princess He Xiao. He'd been raised to filial piety. Hell, his personal name—like hers—meant that very thing. Besides, he loved her, despite her autocratic and tyrannical ways.

Obediently, Yi Xiao told Burton, "My grandmother is sending me to America and wishes you to transport me."

Burton, who'd obviously understood already, frowned. "Madam Lang, the *Henrietta Marie* is a cargo ship. We've carried passengers in steerage before—twenty American dollars a head—but it's hardly the place for a young noble like your grandson. Surely you can find another, more comfortable, way to get him where he needs to go?"

The suggestion made Yi Xiao scoff, but he didn't say what he was thinking. He'd spent most of the last two years cultivating his Self on Heng Shan's peaks. Alone except for his chosen master, he'd sat in a cave, or atop the mountain or even in the middle of a racing stream. All to teach his soul the ways of the *Dao*. A ship's steerage, dark and crowded though it might be, would be unpleasant but survivable.

Rather than explain, all Yi Xiao asked was, "You've carried passengers that way before. Have any died?"

"I'm pleased to say they have not."

"If they can survive the journey I can as well. My family is, as you say, one of the noblest. We are not pampered pets who can hardly bear sunlight, much less a few days...."

"Months. The trip is at least two and half months, if the winds and weather are with us."

"Months, then. I won't pretend it will be easy, yet I can do what I must. Little though I might wish to." The last escaped Yi Xiao's lips before he could hold them back, eliciting a glare from his grandmother. He flinched, adding, "When do you sail?"

"I plan on leaving in a day or so. The weather may or may not cooperate but if you expect to leave with us, you'd better be on board before then. Time and tide wait for no man, no matter how noble his blood."

OOO

With an agreement made, Madam Lang was kind enough to offer Burton dinner and a place to sleep. He gladly accepted; he hadn't eaten for hours now and he needed a rest. Besides, his curiosity was up. There had to be a reason Madam Lang was sending her grandson away, so clearly against his wishes. Burton wanted to know why. It didn't matter to him, but it was a mystery and experience had taught him carting a mystery around unexamined was how one found oneself neck deep in trouble.

Dinner was a great pot of boiling soup set up in the middle of the table. Everyone, from the smallest and most excitable daughter to Madam Lang herself, was responsible for dropping raw meats and vegetables into the pot and retrieving what they wanted to eat. There were odd sauces; raw egg, soy sauce, vinegar and many different spices. Burton made mental notes. He doubted his sister back home would care for this style of eating but he might persuade his crew to try it sometime.

As for the company, it was strangely familiar and comfortable. He'd always found his loud, boisterous and obstreperous crew to be better companions than his own flesh and blood. The Langs weren't nearly as crude or socially inept as the crew of the *Henrietta Marie* but they had their own ways. The children—easily half a dozen little girls—ran around the dining hall, babbling loud and fast about their lessons and their play. Meanwhile their elders talked over them, ignoring them except when they nearly pulled the pot down atop themselves.

The previous generation were only a little quieter. They kept Yi Xiao busy, asking him all sorts of odd questions about what he'd been doing. Burton didn't understand what 'cultivating' meant, nor why cinnabar fields were important, but he could tell it was impressive; at least to Yi Xiao's many sisters. Burton wondered how the family kept them straight, for each and every ones' names began with 'Yi'. It was apparently a tradition, where children of the same generation bore the same syllable in their name.

As for Yi Xiao's father, mother, elder brother and sister-in-law, they seemed busy going over some sort of engine plans. They barely acknowledged Burton's existence, not rudely, but because they were focused on their own interests. Burton, whose youngest brother had a similar bent, would have understood.

There were two members of the household whose presence pleased and confused Burton. Yi Xiao's English tutor was, apparently, a member of the family, despite her obviously British origin. Red-haired and grey-eyed, Grace Smythe-Barnes was governess, secretary and all around household assistant. Ordinarily, Burton would never expect to find a white woman working for a Chinese family, no matter how noble they obviously were.

The woman's daughter, Yi Jin, explained everything. The girl was obviously half-Chinese, her light brown hair and slender hazel eyes combined with ivory skin and high-cheekbones. It didn't take Burton long to realize she was Yi Xiao's half-sister, a situation some might find scandalous. Burton, knowing Chinese society as he did, was only surprised Mr. Lang's second wife was white, not that he had one at all.

As they ate, Burton answered Yi Jin's many questions about his travels, which in turn elicited an apology from her mother. "Please don't let her overwhelm you." The woman gave Yi Jin a warning look, adding, "She can be terribly pushy sometimes."

"I'm just practicing my English, mother. Like you wanted me to."

Burton chuckled and waved off the apology. "She's also being kind, keeping the English speaker entertained. I do know a bit of Chinese, but not nearly enough for a proper conversation."

"Even so...."

"Even so, how about I ask a possibly rude and pushy question myself." The second Mrs. Lang smiled, waving for him to go on. "I realize it may

" ... IMPRESSIVE; AT LEAST TO YI XIAO'S MANY SISTERS. "

be family business and something you'd prefer not to discuss, but given I have to transport him; why is Yi Xiao's grandmother sending him off with a flea in his ear? Did he embarrass the family somehow?"

Burton knew the question was risky. It was obvious from the elderly matriarch's attitude that her plans were secret. But he'd once had to race all the way from Bangkok to London, pursued by pirates and fake officials. He didn't like mysterious treasures with unknown troubles attached. He still didn't know what'd been in that box, either.

It was Madam Lang who answered her English far better than she'd pretended earlier. "It is a family affair, Captain. Yi Xiao, himself, has done nothing wrong. But there are those who would use him to bring trouble to others."

Seeing that was all he'd be told, Burton was about to try a different tack when Yi Xiao interrupted, frowning puzzledly. "What did you mean, 'flea in my ear'?"

Chuckling, Yi Xiao's... second mother? step-mother? aunt?... told him, "It's an idiom, Xiao Xiao. It means to send someone off with a rebuke." She added for Burton's benefit, "The whole family understands formal English, but idioms like those are difficult to teach."

Almost perkily, Yi Xiao agreed. "Like what you said earlier. The word you said I should ask my tutor about." Before Burton could stop him, he turned to the second Mrs. Lang. "Sod, I think it was. Short for sodomite?"

Burton felt his cheeks go bright red as Mrs. Lang turned a hard, cold, look on him. "I'm a sailor," he said weakly. "I was upset."

There was an odd and nearly identical expression on both Madam Lang's face and Yi Xiao's. A faint trembling of the lips suggested they were scant inches from bursting into laughter. The second Mrs. Lang glanced from one to the other, lips tight. Finally she shook her head. "Yi Xiao, you may ask Mr. Burton to explain the meaning of the word later when you are in less polite company than this."

Softly, the old lady murmured, "Cutting the sleeve isn't quite as impolite, grandson. But I wouldn't suggest using that phrase where you're going, either."

Comprehension dawned in Yi Xiao's eyes. "Oh. Oh, I see. I had a feeling it was something rude, given the circumstances. But he did tell me to ask you, Mama Grace."

"I'm sure he did. I also sure you knew you shouldn't." Mrs. Lang sighed, catching hold of a rapidly moving girl as she passed. "Take warning, Captain Burton. Mischief does not run in this family, it trots, gallops and capers through it."

The conversation turned to other, less significant things, but Burton found himself wondering just what he was getting himself into, transporting a man like Yi Xiao anywhere.

○○○

It was impossible to sleep. The shock of his grandmother's plans left Yi Xiao confused and frightened. He was painfully conscious that he shouldn't be so disturbed. "Master says, confusion is as natural as order. Move with it and it will come to rest," he reminded himself, sitting in a quiet corner of the garden.

He wished he understood why he was being sent away; with or without a flea in his ear. Grandmother had made it clear it wasn't his actions that had brought about his exile, but neither had she told him what had. She was still angry at him for leaving his sabre behind, even though a priest of the Wind and Rain sect had no need of such things.

Yi Xiao's meditation was interrupted by movement on the path beyond his hiding place. Burton, clumsy and unafraid, coming back from a trip to the toilet. No surprise. The foreigner had drunk several whole pots of tea at dinner. Not to mention eaten far more food than anyone Yi Xiao had seen before.

Burton stopped in his tracks and a faint sound rustled. Yi Xiao didn't move, but he focused his *qi*, tuning his awareness to the world around him. Now he knew there was a third man in the garden, creeping stealthily through the underbrush towards the house.

The stranger was using his own inner awareness to help him find his way past the house guard. No doubt that was how he'd gotten so far past Yi Xiao. Admittedly, Yi Xiao's inattention had helped, yet only a trained warrior could have managed such a feat even assisted by Yi Xiao's distraction.

There were places where Yi Xiao would have ignored an intruder. His grandmother's Shanghai home was not one of them. He stood, intending to interrupt the stranger's slow progress, but Burton got there first. "Hey! Are you supposed to be here?" When Burton reached out to grab the man, the stranger sent him flying. He lay, gasping for air, while the stranger dropped a heel into his sternum.

As the Captain stared blearily at his attacker, muttering Yi Xiao's name, the man drew his sword, placing it at Burton's throat.

Yi Xiao moved quickly, fingers striking the intruder's spine, the back of his ear and collarbone. Immediately, the man went still, though his voice did not. "How dare you lay hands on me?"

The voice and arrogance were familiar. Unimpressed, Yi Xiao retorted, "You're the one sneaking around grandmother's garden, Zhu Zhu. What did you expect would happen?" He helped Captain Burton to his feet. "Go inside and tell a servant to fetch my grandmother. Tell them I said we have an important guest."

"How about I give him a taste of what he gave me instead?"

"Do as I say. Now." Yi Xiao deepened his voice, gazing levelly at the Captain. Somehow, by some miracle of sense, Burton stopped arguing. Maybe nearly getting his spine snapped and his throat cut had had a salutatory effect on his mobile tongue. He hurried inside silently.

Once Burton had gone, Yi Xiao returned his attention to his prisoner, undoing the paralysis. "Now, cousin, I'm sure you have an explanation for this. I'm equally sure you think it's a good one. I'm not certain my grandmother will agree."

OOO

Ordinarily, Burton would never have walked away from a fight. The blow to his head must have shaken him up. Well, that and Yi Xiao's resemblance to his grandmother went further than skin deep. The youngster had an unexpectedly commanding side to him, one that defied argument.

Finding a servant took several minutes. Getting her to understand the situation was only resolved by the second Mrs. Lang's arrival. "Whatever is going on out here? Mr. Burton, you're making quite a fuss. Is something wrong?"

"There's an intruder who looks just like Yi Xiao."

Burton was exaggerating but the resemblance was marked. They were both fine-featured, with long noses and thick brows. The newcomer wore his hair in the same style as most Manchus, but his forehead was covered in a thick dark stubble, as if he hadn't had a chance to shave recently. The greatest difference lay in attitude. The stranger had an arrogant, self-assured, air that Yi Xiao lacked. Yi Xiao's voice of command aside, the boy always seemed to be sniggering up his sleeve at the world.

"An intruder? Who looks like Yi Xiao?" The second Mrs. Lang gave quick, sharp, orders to the servant who immediately ran off into the twisted maze of hallways. Then the woman returned her attention to Burton. "How was he dressed?"

Ruefully, Burton admitted, "I didn't notice much else about him. A hooded robe over the usual street clothes, I think. Something grey, maybe a black vest?"

"Nothing embroidered? No dragons?"

Burton tried to think. "No. Nothing like that. He looked like a merchant. Respectable. Even staid... aside from a regrettable tendency to throw people over their shoulders."

Madam Lang came down the hallway, her spry steps belying her age. She barely gave her daughter-in-law a glance. "Where is my grandson and the intruder?"

"Still out back, I think." There was a shout and a crash, quickly followed by the sound of flesh striking flesh. A moment later Yi Xiao came flipping down the hallway, calling back something incomprehensible. Whatever language he spoke, it was neither formal Chinese nor the informal dock-tainted dialect Burton understood best.

The other man skidded down the hallway, expression calm and hard as he aimed a blow at Yi Xiao's chin. It missed, for Yi Xiao evaded him with that same slippery snake movement from earlier. Burton had never seen anyone fight the way Yi Xiao did but it was effective, albeit aggravating for the one trying to hit him.

Blow after blow narrowly missed as Yi Xiao called out what sounded like insults. His opponent didn't like them, that was certain. His nose flared and his lips tightened every time Yi Xiao opened his mouth. Yet throughout all this he stayed calm, just shifted, struck and kicked so fast his limbs were a blur in the dimly lit hallway.

For some reason Yi Xiao seemed unwilling to strike his opponent. He kept his hands safely behind his back, as if to keep himself from instinctively reacting to the stranger's attacks. "What's the matter, Zhu Zhu? Can't move fast enough?" He was grinning dangerously, a daredevil flirting with the edge of disaster.

Madam Lang had had enough. "Stop this nonsense right this minute," she ordered calmly in Chinese. "Both of you."

Yi Xiao might have been enjoying the fight but he obeyed immediately. The intruder was less submissive. He used the moment of Yi Xiao's distraction to land a blow straight in the middle of the young man's belly.

Some men would have fallen over immediately, the breath knocked out of them. All Yi Xiao allowed himself was a soft, "Oof." Then another and another as his attacker let loose with a flurry of blows that ought to have broken every rib he had. Burton was impressed. Most men would have been falling over their own feet under such punishment.

Madam Lang smacked the intruder's head with her cane. "Young man, you will cease this behavior this minute." Her tone was the very one Burton's mother used when her children had gone too far. It had the same effect, ending the game immediately.

"Aunt He Xiao! He attacked me first. After sending the foreigner after me!" The young man sounded whiney, even to himself and he readjusted his tone, bowing slightly to Madam Lang. "I'm incognito, I admit it, but he of all people should have recognized me."

"Cousin, your hood hid your face. I didn't recognize you until after I'd disabled you." Yi Xiao brushed himself off, gesture resembling a cat cleaning himself after a clumsy tumble. "And our guest didn't attack you."

Burton almost spoke up, but a sharp glance from Madam Lang stopped him. The old lady was a fearsome figure. If she'd been a man, she'd be Emperor. Instead of arguing, he stepped back and let her do her work.

"Daughter. Take the Captain back to his room. I shall handle these two miscreants." When the stranger looked offended, she added, "You broke into my garden and started a fight with my guest. Do not dare pretend you have no responsibility for what happened."

Burton raised a hand. "Madam Lang, does this have to do with my upcoming trip, and my cargo?" When the old woman raised a brow, he added, "If so, I have some part in this matter. Besides, your nephew did nearly break my back throwing me over his shoulder."

After several long seconds of careful thought, Madam Lang said, "It isn't fair to set you a task that might turn dangerous. Ignorance may be bliss, but it is an unaffordable pleasure right now."

Returning her attention to the others, the old lady ordered, "Come with me. Explanations are in order." Then, without bothering to make sure she was obeyed, she walked away, cane thumping on the floor softly as she went.

OOO

Yi Xiao walked beside his cousin, deliberately aping the other man's stately mannerisms. Zhu Zhu always was a trifle full of himself even when they'd been children. Back then, Zhu Zhu hadn't realized just how much of Yi Xiao's imitation was mild mockery. Now, he was deeply annoyed.

"Stop teasing your cousin," Grandmother Lang said sharply. "I don't need to look to know you are. You always do."

Knowing he'd been pinned to the wall and hung up to dry, Yi Xiao simply said, "Yes, Ma'am. Sorry, Zhu Zhu." He sneaked a look at his cousin and was surprised and pleased by a momentary look of glee turned his way. So Zhu Zhu had learned a little bit of humor after all. Not enough to make him any less stiff and self-important, but a little.

To Yi Xiao's surprise, his grandmother didn't take them to her office. Instead she led them downstairs into the practice room. His cousin was equally surprised, asking, "Auntie, are we to duel to settle our differences?"

It was a fair question; she'd had them do so before, after all. But now Yi Xiao was a priest of the Wind and Rain and his cousin was practically untouchable. Yi Xiao meant it when he'd said he hadn't realized who Zhu Zhu was until after he'd struck. Once he'd recognized his cousin all he could do was evade. Which, fortunately, was one of the first things his master back in Heng Shan had taught him. Zhu Zhu's martial arts had improved immensely since they'd last met.

"Not at all." Grandmother Lang took the only seat in the room and gestured for everyone else to come closer. "I want privacy and this is the most secure room in the house. After all, we practice our secret technique here."

Burton coughed. "Err. Secret technique?"

Zhu Zhu looked disdainful and tightened his lips while Yi Xiao looked away innocently. He wasn't sure his grandmother was right to bring this outsider into their business but he certainly wasn't going to be the one to explain the secrets of the martial world.

To his deep surprise, however, Grandmother Lang told the man, "Our family practices a martial art called Blade of the White Wolf. As one of the leading families of the *jianghu*, it's our duty to use what we learn here to guide and protect our country."

A confused expression crossed Burton's face. "Leading families of the rivers and lakes? I don't understand."

It took Yi Xiao a moment to realize the trouble. "The word *jianghu* translates literally to rivers and lakes, but it's an idiom meaning the martial world. There are families, clans and societies who train their members to fight or use other techniques." He had a feeling—based on what second mama had taught him—that Burton either wouldn't understand or would scoff at those skills. Given they didn't have time to explain, it was easier to just gloss over the whole thing.

When it looked like Burton was going to press for more, Zhu Zhu interrupted. "Foreigner, you're allowed to be here only because Imperial Princess He Xiao says so. May I suggest you shut your mouth and use your ears to actually learn something?"

The Captain turned a quick look Grandmother Lang's way. "Imperial Princess? Impressive. I figured you were important, but not that important. Are you the Emperor's sister, then?"

Before Zhu Zhu could show his anger at Burton's lack of manners, Grandmother Lang told the man, "I am a great deal too old for that. I am his father's sister." She made a gesture at Zhu Zhu, adding, "Allow me to handle the situation, nephew. I would much rather know what you are doing here, rather than heading for Beijing. Even if you have been irresponsible enough to spend your days carousing in brothels and wandering the cities incognito, you cannot be so blind to your duty as to remain away while your father lies gravely ill."

Zhu Zhu flushed bright red. "I had more purpose to my wandering than carousing," he said softly. "And I've been trying to get home, I swear it. My enemies have blocked my path at every turn."

As if to prove Zhu Zhu's point, a servant came running into the room. "Madam Lang! Madam Lang! General Hwei is in the main hall. He demands your presence!"

The news didn't surprise Grandmother Lang. Her lips tightened as she told the servant, "Provide the General with tea. Tell him he must be patient with an old woman woken suddenly from sleep. It may take me some time to grant him the audience he desires."

Once the servant had run off, Grandmother Lang turned to Zhu Zhu. "We must act fast and you must do as I say, without hesitation or argument." Seeing Zhu Zhu about to do that very thing, she tapped him on the nose with her index finger. "If you would reach your father before he dies, you must obey me."

Unwillingly, Zhu Zhu inclined his head. "What do I do?"

"Let your hair hang loose. It's fortunate you haven't had time to properly shave your scalp. Also, remove your robes."

That nearly made Zhu Zhu rebel, but Yi Xiao interrupted. "And I cut my forelocks and give him my clothes?" Now he understood the plan and the part he was to play.

"Good boy. Yes." Madam Lang turned to Captain Burton. "You've guessed?"

"I think so. He's the heir, Prince Yi Zhu, isn't he? And this General Hwei wants to keep him from reaching the Emperor before he dies."

Yi Xiao ignored the discussion, preparing himself for his rôle. With only the slightest regret, he began hacking his forelocks down as short as he could. There wasn't time to shave, but it didn't matter. The enemy would think his cousin was trying to disguise himself as a Han.

"I don't understand," Zhu Zhu muttered, untying his braid and spreading his hair down his shoulders. "What is she up to?"

Yi Xiao grinned, taking off his robe. "It's simple. You're running away to sea." As his cousin stared at him in outraged disbelief, he added, "Or, rather, I am for you."

Zhu Zhu's glare was immediately distracted by the sight of Yi Xiao's naked shoulders. The mark of the storm, painful proof of his training, forked its way along his arm and torso. He pointed. "You...."

"Don't you remember I was training on Heng Shan?"

"You never said you were training with the Storm Hermit."

Most people didn't try to learn from the Storm Hermit. It took a great deal of courage to approach her lightning guarded fastness. Yi Xiao, whose courage often masqueraded as foolhardy overconfidence, had been among the few to reach her and the even fewer to convince her to let him learn.

"Now I know why you didn't dare strike me."

"Other than the fact that one doesn't strike the heir?"

"As if that's ever stopped you before."

"It does now and not just because I could kill you," Yi Xiao retorted, sliding into his cousin's robe and pulling the hood over his head. He turned to Grandmother Lang. "Madam...." His voice choked with emotion.

"Be well. Be safe. You have our blessings. Seek our old friend Chang when you reach San Francisco." The old woman handed Yi Xiao a pack, then set a hand in blessing on his head. "Go. General Hwei surely has men watching out for your cousin and you must lead them astray."

ooo

It took Burton embarrassingly long to work out the plan. In his defense, he was a foreigner, a mere ship's Captain, with no contacts among the high and mighty of Chinese society. Yet the situation was now painfully obvious. Even knowing as little as he did about Chinese politics he could guess the First Prince was in danger. Wandering around anonymously, he'd stayed away too long, giving his enemies time to take advantage of their Emperor's weakness. If Yi Zhu couldn't get back to court before his father died, he'd lose both throne and life.

It only took a few minutes to get to the other end of the passage beneath the Lang family's house. Dimly lit by Yi Xiao's lamp, there was something unnerving about the shadows and shifting breeze as it drifted past Burton's face. When they climbed a narrow set of steps into a small cemetery and a dozen bats dove past them, Burton came inches from telling Yi Xiao just what the boy could do with the pretty and valuable jade amulet Madam Lang had paid for his passage.

Fortunately for Burton's future bank account, Yi Xiao said sympathetically, "You don't have to take me if you're better off not accepting this job. I'll think no less of you if you tell me to find another way to reach America. Nor will I mind if you keep Grandmother's amulet. You didn't sign up for Chinese politics."

There were plenty of things Burton hadn't signed up for. However, "I accepted payment and agreed to the terms. Jake Burton keeps his word without needing it written down."

A quick, relieved, smile crossed Yi Xiao's face. The kid had been worried and rightly so. He was in a world of trouble by no fault of his own. None of this was fair. Yi Xiao hadn't done anything—aside from strongly resemble his cousin—to be forced into self-exile.

When Burton expressed sympathy, Yi Xiao shrugged it off. "I obey my family's needs. Besides, I can seek the *Dao* wherever I go."

Although Burton didn't understand at all, the question of what *Dao* was and why it mattered had to wait. The youngster strode along the middle of the road, making no effort to sneak around. He could have been a wanderer seeking a place to sleep or a messenger with no time to waste. Yi Zhu's enemies, however, knew what they were looking for.

Several dozen men stepped out of the shadows just as they neared the entrance to Old Town. Most wore the simple dark-blue uniforms of Chinese foot-soldiers; short tunics with a single character on them and trousers stuffed into padded boots. Armed with short spears, their grim expressions told Burton they weren't looking for a dance.

Yi Xiao paused as a broad shouldered man of medium height sauntered into sight. He had hard, grim, features, with a greying mustache and equally greying queue beneath an elegant black cap. His dark robes were the sort Burton had seen high-level officials wear, with a heavily embroidered square at the chest. Burton didn't know what the symbol meant but he knew this man was trouble. Big trouble.

The man sneered at the sight of them, stalking forward silently. "The General and I have been looking for you for quite some time, your Highness," he said in Chinese. "And here I find you consorting with foreign devils? Really, Yi Zhu, it's men like him who shamed your father."

"Hey. Don't blame me for the Brits," Burton snapped. He didn't know if the man spoke English but he couldn't help interrupting.

Both men ignored him, busy circling each other while the soldiers gathered round. While Burton tried to work out the best path for their escape, Yi Xiao said, in perfect imitation of his cousin's haughty tones, "Your master's failure to protect our waterways allowed the British to shame us, Colonel Tsang."

"What he said," Burton added, stepping closer to one of the guards. Immediately the man's spear sliced downwards, blocking his path. "Hey, careful. Those things are sharp."

Meanwhile, Tsang was growling furiously, cursing and threatening to feed his enemy his entrails. "If I could see you face the death of a thousand cuts, I would, you turtle dung!" At the same time he raised his hands, crooking his fingers in a strange gesture. Burton blinked, almost certain a flicker of purple fire crackled around the man's gauntlets.

"Didn't Colonel Bianshi try that last year? The youngest son of the Langs removed his head for him." Yi Xiao took a step backwards, so he was close to Burton. In English he said, "Don't interfere. Get me to the ship after he's gone."

Burton didn't understand, but agreed. Yi Xiao had some plan up his sleeve it seemed. All Burton could do was go along with it. Even if he had his pistol the best he could do was injure the enemy. A bullet might make it through the man's armor but it wouldn't do much damage. Nor could Burton fight so many people. Not even with the impressively skilled Yi Xiao there to help.

ooo

Colonel Tsang was stronger than he'd been the one time Yi Xiao had watched him fight. A follower of the Black Thunder sect, the Colonel transformed his inner energies to a particularly virulent form of negative *qi*. It was one step short of black magic and despised by most inhabitants of the martial world. Sadly, it was not yet illegal.

"Dare you raise your hand to me?" Yi Xiao demanded, keeping his voice deep. The Colonel had yet to realize he was attacking the wrong man and he needed to keep it that way. If Tsang, and thus his master Hwei, could be persuaded that he'd murdered the Prince he wouldn't go after the Yi Xiao traveling to Beijing with Grandmother Lang.

"Why not? You're a vagabond. A poorly dressed madman who attacked me in the streets." Colonel Tsang smiled at Yi Xiao's wide-eyed expression,

"Yes, you fool. You thought your disguise amusing, no doubt. Thought its anonymity would protect you. But it also means no one will know you when you die. I'll leave you in the dirt for the scavengers."

Before Yi Xiao could open his mouth to argue, Tsang struck, hands covered with the dark energies of his *qi*. It seared through Yi Xiao, intensely cold and intensely painful. If he hadn't spent the last two years learning to redirect the Storm Hermit's lightning, he'd have been knocked unconscious in seconds.

Grounding the energies, Yi Xiao let loose a scream that probably woke the entire neighborhood. Not that anyone would be fool enough to try and find out what was going on. Those outside the martial world generally knew better than to poke their noses into it.

"Hah! Your skill is weak as ever!" Colonel Tsang didn't waste time gloating. He caught Yi Xiao's face by the jaw, sending his dark *qi* into his victim's body with furious glee. He didn't notice the same energy dissipating into the ground, redirected there by Yi Xiao's less visible aura.

Even partially defended, Yi Xiao was in agony. He'd experienced worse but not by much. Still, it was almost time to implement the next stage of his plan. He'd have to make it look good. Tsang wasn't a fool and if he noticed anything wrong about his victim's 'death' he'd surely realize how he'd been tricked.

Yi Xiao struggled to break free, grabbing at his attacker's wrist and kicking. He tried to wrap his legs around his enemy's torso, as if to take him down that way, only to find himself slammed down onto his back. Burton shouted incoherently and he was desperately glad the American didn't forget himself and use Yi Xiao's real name.

Help, unwanted and unneeded, came from another direction. Gasping, throat burning, lungs bursting, Yi Xiao barely heard the sound like a thousand arrows slicing the air. A willow leaf sabre struck the ground inches from his left hand, its curved surface engraved with ancient characters.

Yi Xiao ignored the blade in favor of trying to escape his attacker. Not because he wanted to but because that was what was expected of him. Except a moment later he was free, sprawled across the cobblestones, choking and wheezing as a white-clad figure whirled around the Colonel.

Blinking, he stared at the stranger, watching her long dark hair float on the breeze, entwined with robes of the finest opalescent silk, her face hidden by an equally diaphanous veil. "Take your sabre," she ordered, keeping Colonel Tsang's dark aura from touching her with a delicate gesture. It wasn't as easy as she made it look. Her lips were tight, her jaw clenched

" A WILLOW LEAF SABER STRUCK THE GROUND... "

against the pain. "Defend yourself!"

The sabre was, indeed, Yi Xiao's; the one he'd left buried in a stone on the highest peak of Heng Shan. He wanted to demand how she'd found it, how she'd managed to get it free and, more importantly, why she'd brought it back to the man who didn't want it. That would mean admitting he wasn't who he pretended to be. Right that moment he didn't dare.

"My sabre?" he croaked, watching her fight with a blade as slim and shining as she was. Elegant sweeps and strikes sent Colonel Tsang's attacks flying harmlessly away. She was good, though not quite as good as he'd been. "It's not my sabre."

"Of course it's your sabre. Whose else would it be?" Tsang got a strike in during her moment of distraction, sending her flying.

Yi Xiao rose to his feet. "It looks like... Yi Xiao's... sabre. But... he's given... it up." He hoped she'd believe him. He didn't have time to deal with whatever troubles she brought with her.

The woman dodged the Colonel's next blow, but she was starting to tire. Redirecting power like Tsang's took mental strength. "Given it up? Nonsense!"

Once again Tsang slammed his open palm into the woman's shoulder. "Fool girl," he growled. "Don't interfere in my business!" She fell, landing in a heap and struggling to rise. It was obvious from the blood staining her shoulder she could not. Black energy bubbled around the injury, stinking of decay and death.

"Burton, take care of her," Yi Xiao called out. He had to deal with Tsang and get the girl to safety quickly. Injured as she was, she didn't have much time before Tsang's poisonous *qi* killed her. Regretfully, Yi Xiao took his sabre. "Master says, when life is endangered, do what must be done," he reminded himself. Then he loosed a series of slashing cuts that forced Tsang backwards.

"White Wolf style, Yi Zhu? It won't save you. You can't have mastered it." The Colonel's dark aura sparked with purple shafts of lightning that Yi Xiao parried and redirected easily.

"Miss? Miss, are you all right?"

Knowing the girl couldn't last long, Yi Xiao began the elaborate pattern of strikes characteristic of the White Wolf Blade. Created by an illustrious ancestress, they required both speed and agility to perfect. Yi Xiao had abandoned the style in favor of his master's, but the skills he'd learned had not faded.

At the same time, Tsang drew his dark aura together, entire body crackling with black-tinted lightning. He was as good as Yi Xiao, certainly as fast, and the power he'd gathered would obliterate the *qi* of any living thing it touched. It was a race now. Yi Xiao couldn't attack and defend at the same time, but neither could Colonel Tsang.

Fortune, more than anything else, was on Yi Xiao's side. He flung himself forward, blade flashing as he struck, and reached Tsang just seconds before the Colonel could unleash his full power. Without hesitation he thrust his sabre deep, driving it into the man's belly and up into his heart.

OOO

The fight left Burton near speechless. He'd heard rumors of strange powers and magics, but he'd never seen such fireworks close up. Nor had he seen bloodlust like Yi Xiao's before and he hoped never to see it again. It almost made him run from the whole mess. Only the girl, lips covered in froth and body shuddering as the poison worked through her system, kept him where he was. She was so young and helpless, a mere child in desperate straits.

Knowing Colonel Tsang's death would bring more trouble; Burton hoisted the girl in his arms and shouted to Yi Xiao, "We have to get out of here!" He just hoped he wasn't carrying a corpse who hadn't realized she was dead yet.

"We will," Yi Xiao agreed, pulling his weapon from his victim's chest and cleaned it on Tsang's robe. Turning, he glared at his enemy's soldiers. "You know who I am?"

They were staring, stunned and terrified by the look in the man's eyes. Not that Burton blamed them. They could easily be Yi Xiao's next victims. They dropped to their knees and began to kowtow. "Please, your Highness. Forgive us! He was our commander. We were bound to obey!"

"Go to Madam Lang and surrender yourselves to her. Tell her what happened and what I told you. Assist her return to Beijing safely and your sins may be forgiven." The order sent the soldiers scurrying off rapidly.

Yi Xiao snatched up the girl's sword and headed the other way, not bothering to make sure Burton followed. "Bring her along. I'll see to her injuries aboard ship. Can we leave immediately?"

"I think so. If the winds are with us, at least." Burton didn't like rushing off so quickly but he could tell this mess was going to spill onto him and his ship if he stayed. "By noon, I hope."

"The wind will be with us. I promise." Yi Xiao's expression, usually flighty and mischievous, was as stern and commanding as his Imperial cousin's. "Colonel Tsang is not the only one whose *qi* commands the elements."

"What was all that about, anyway? I've never seen anything like it."

Yi Xiao's old mischief returned in his voice. "If you ride the rivers and lakes you'll see it all the time. Would you like to learn?"

Burton thought about it. Thought about his ship and the nice, simple, life he led. Then, without hesitation, he said, "No. Not at all. I have better things to do than swinging a sword or turning people into lightning rods."

With a laugh, Yi Xiao said, "To tell the truth, Captain Burton. So do I." His expression turned distant as they headed towards the *Henrietta Marie*. "Master says, a true disciple of the *Dao* can find balance no matter where they are. Perhaps, if I'm fortunate, I will find it in America as readily as I would have found it here."

Chapter 2: Water –
Continuing towards Greater Order

It took days for Gan Han to realize she was at sea. Dazed and in pain as she was, it was about all she could do to keep from crying. A warrior of the Hua did not cry. The heir to the family's Lotus Blossom technique most especially did not cry. She refused to admit she was crying.

Her healer didn't help her mood. His utter refusal to admit to being Yi Xiao was bad enough. His cheery sense of humor only made her angry. The fact that he'd rescued her from a fight she probably shouldn't have joined was embarrassing. His calm disregard for her modesty as he healed her was humiliating. If she could have risen from her bunk and cut him down, she would have.

As the pain from her injury finally subsided and Gan Han realized where she was, she came the closest she'd come to panicking in her life. When her healer entered the tiny and horribly dark room, she attacked immediately. "Where have you taken me, you bastard?"

The man caught her arm and forced her back into her bed without effort. "Now, now. You're not strong enough for such nonsense."

"Answer me, Yi Xiao!"

"I'm just an itinerant priest," he said, checking her pulse. "Nobody important. Why do you want this Yi Xiao, anyway? Did he run away from marrying you? Silly of him if he did; you're far too pretty to leave behind, even with that scar."

Gan Han traced the twisted knot of flesh that marked her from cheekbone to chin. Then she slapped the man as hard as she was able. It was too dark to see much, but she knew it wasn't nearly hard enough, leaving barely a mark on his cheek. "How dare you insult me?"

"No, really, it's no insult," he insisted. "That scar healed well and the rest of your face is quite attractive."

The flattery made Gan Han nervous and she grabbed her coverlet, pulling it up over herself. It was pointless modesty. He'd surely seen far more of her than any man but a husband had a right to. Admittedly, it'd been to save her life, but that didn't make it any less embarrassing.

To her great relief, Yi Xiao didn't press the point. Instead, he set a bundle of cloth on the end of her bunk. "Having healed you, I now prescribe sunlight and fresh sea air. Both of which, I note, we have in abundance. You'll want to dress warmly. Even in full daylight, the wind is strong and cold out there. You can use that stick if you need something to lean on. Be careful coming outside. Captain Burton claims the sea is mild and pleasant at the moment. An inexperienced sea traveler, however, might not agree."

With that, the idiot left the room.

OOO

Sea travel was unexpectedly pleasant. Yi Xiao hadn't admitted it before, but he'd been a little worried. He'd heard travelers' stories about seasickness and difficulty walking. Perhaps it was his training, tied as it was to wind and storm that gave him the advantage.

Having done what he could for the young lady—whose name he still didn't know—Yi Xiao joined Captain Burton at the rear of the *Henrietta Marie*. The sun was warm against his back, the scent of the sea air was a heady mix of salt and fish and the cool wind ruffled his now collar-length hair.

"I thought you said you were going to convince her to come out?" Captain Burton asked. He was dressed much like Yi Xiao right then; a light linen shirt and trousers and a kerchief to protect his head from the sunlight. It was odd clothing to Yi Xiao, but it meant he fit in. Captain Burton's crew was a motley bunch from all corners of the globe. A Chinese sailor dressed in European clothes didn't stand out at all.

Yi Xiao leaned over the railing to see if the young lady was there yet. "I'm not sure she will," he admitted. "She doesn't seem to like me much."

"She doesn't trust you, you mean. Not that I blame her."

Since no one could blame someone in their guest's circumstances for distrusting a chancy fellow like Yi Xiao, he didn't argue. Of course, that was the way Yi Xiao preferred it. She was, as he'd said, attractive enough, but he didn't need the distraction. She was a problem and not just because he'd had to detoxify Colonel Tsang's dark aura from her system. The fact that she'd been looking for him made things even more awkward.

"I just wish I knew what she wanted of me."

"Is she your fiancée?" Burton held up his left ring finger for some reason. "Your people have arranged marriages, right?"

Yi Xiao was almost certain she wasn't. "My grandmother is autocratic and given to making decisions about our lives without consulting us. But she generally tells us her intentions, once she'd made up her mind."

"Perhaps you met her before and made her think you'd marry her?"

Now that was ridiculous. "That girl is barely fifteen. A mere child. She shouldn't even be out on her own—daughter of the martial world or no." He didn't mention he'd chosen to enter that world at fourteen, excited by the danger and eager to prove his skill against all comers.

"Juliet Capulet was thirteen, you know." Burton grinned, adding, "That's Shakespeare, in case your second mother never taught it to you."

"Mama Grace is English, I'll remind you. And Romeo and Juliet was set in Italy, at a time when such things were common," Yi Xiao pointed out dryly. "I admit, Grandmother did marry at fifteen, but that was because she wouldn't stop pestering her father." Grandmother Lang had loved her husband from the first, even after her father-in-law, the traitor Heshen, had been forced to commit suicide. It was her devotion and stubborn will that had saved the family from disgrace. That and the fact that she'd terrified her brother, the Jiaqing Emperor.

Burton chuckled. "I admit, if a lady like your grandmother wants something it'd take a pretty strong will to deny her." He returned his attention to the question at hand. "What about that sword she tried to give you? Is that what your grandmother meant by willow leaf knife?"

Yi Xiao sighed at the memory. He'd a feeling he wasn't going to be forgiven for leaving his weapon behind anytime soon. "It's a sabre, not a sword, but yes."

The distinction puzzled Burton immensely. "I don't understand."

"Swords like the one the young lady carries are called *jian*. They're two-edged and are considered weapons for elite warriors. My weapon, being single-edged, is a *dao* and is more common; a soldier's weapon."

"Oh. I see. Like a cavalry sword, back home?"

"I'm not sure. I've never seen western swords." Yi Xiao set aside his curiosity regretfully. He was not yet far enough along his path to think about such things. "Not that it matters."

"Your patient may disagree on that subject," Burton offered wryly. "Speaking of whom...." He pointed at the young woman stumbling out into the light.

Yi Xiao somersaulted over the railing and landed beside her. Dressed now in clothing much like his own, wrapped in a warm jacket and clutching her stick in a desperate attempt to stay upright, she looked a little like a street beggar. Her hair was a tangled mess and her eyes showed a mix of fear and anger. "You could have waited for me."

"I thought you'd prefer to dress alone."

"Why? You've seen it all." Her tone was sharp and bitter. The voice of one who wanted to believe she didn't care.

"I haven't, though. Just your shoulder. Hardly enough to mention." Yi Xiao helped her to the railing and pointed towards the horizon. "If you feel seasick, look out as far as you can. It'll help."

Annoyed, the girl snapped, "I was born on a boat, you bastard. I don't get seasick."

"I see." Yi Xiao considered the information, trying to think where he'd met her and what he'd done to set her after him. Realizing he still didn't know who she was, he asked, "So, what's your name? Unless I'm seriously mistaken, we haven't been introduced."

"I am Xihua Gan Han. We may not have met, but you surely know my name, Yi Xiao."

The family, at least, was familiar. "While I don't recognize you at all, I have to guess you're a member of the Death Flower clan?" Gan Han could be written as steel lotus, and the Death Flowers all went by such names.

Fury flickered in the back of Gan Han's eyes and she tried to take a step towards him, only to trip and nearly fall. He caught her and helped her grasp the railing. "How dare you not know me? Your name is flung in my face everywhere I turn. Yi Xiao's skill is the deftest. Yi Xiao's arm is the strongest. Yi Xiao's blade is the fastest."

It was an old and familiar song. Once a weapons master gained a reputation every other warrior in the martial world wanted to test themselves against it. Once, and not too long ago, Yi Xiao would have admired Gan Han's dedication. Now all he felt was despair. How was he to leave his past behind when it kept following him?

Calmly, or as calmly as he could, he pointed out, "Yi Xiao hasn't been in the martial world for two years, Lady Gan Han. I doubt he was nearly so great a warrior as to overshadow all who followed him."

She sneered. "Tell that to my mother. To my sisters. They saw you fight, saw you defeat the assassin attacking the Emperor's son just last year. Don't tell me you left the martial world two years ago when the truth is obviously not in you."

Yi Xiao hadn't forgotten the incident but he hated to remember it. His cousin had come looking for him, wanting Yi Xiao to join him on his wanderings. Exhausted and dejected by his lack of progress, Yi Xiao had gone with Yi Zhu to the nearby city of Hunyuan. Things hadn't gone well and Yi Xiao had been forced to kill his cousin's would-be murderer.

"Yi Xiao's actions were shameful," he told the woman grimly. "If he killed a man, even in the Prince's defense, he displayed a deplorable lack of self-control." Just as he had a week earlier, fighting Colonel Tsang. The worst of it was just how much he'd enjoyed the killing. "The martial world is a place of violence and greed. Yi Xiao is better out of it."

The statement clearly infuriated Gan Han. She slapped Yi Xiao, her blow still too weak to so much as mark him. "If that's how Yi Xiao thinks, then you're right. He doesn't deserve the name he made for himself. Fight me. I will prove my blade the strongest and send you on your way."

Yi Xiao raised a brow. He'd seen her skill back in Shanghai and while she was good, she wasn't good enough. Even without his sabre he was still the better fighter. Besides, "I am a mere wanderer, with no title except would-be priest. When this ship reaches San Diego, I will be leaving it and you, to go my own way. I suggest you take your pride and your desire for supremacy back to the martial world where it belongs and leave me to my own destiny."

He could feel her hot eyes on him as he walked away.

○○○

If Gan Han hadn't been so weak she would have argued the point with Yi Xiao long after he'd chose to ignore her. The damage the Black Thunder warrior had done her made it impossible. Even with the poison purified from her system, her physical strength wasn't up to the effort.

She tried exercising her way back to full health, exhausting herself in the process. Yi Xiao protested she wouldn't recover from her injuries any faster, but she refused to listen. The Captain—an annoying Westerner with a constantly moving mouth—tried to block her chosen exercise floor. The sailors, a mixed-bag of men from dozens of seaports, kept getting in her way. None of this stopped her.

It was Gan Han's own body that forced her to accept her limitations. One morning after a particularly difficult exercise, she found herself barely able to crawl out of her bed. Not even massage or sitting in the sun in the only quiet spot aboard ship made her feel any better.

Unable to exercise, she sat at the bow of the ship, enjoying the breeze despite herself. She even controlled her urge to growl when Captain Burton came up beside her with a pot of tea. "Now this better," he said in horribly accented Chinese. "You sit. Rest."

"You degrade our language just by setting it on your lips," she muttered, though she did take the tea. It wasn't very good. Of course, it was probably the low quality leaf they only sold to foreigners.

"If speak English, will be glad to criticize back," Burton retorted. Given she'd already told him she'd never learned his barbaric language and had no desire to do so; she ignored the suggestion, sipping her tea in grim silence.

At last Burton asked, "Why sad?"

"I'm not sad, you foolish Westerner. I'm angry. You and that idiot Yi Xiao practically kidnapped me. Now I won't see China again for weeks!" She corrected herself, remembering what she'd been told. "No, months."

"True, yes." Burton leaned against the railing, watching her thoughtfully. "And sorry for that. But we had to leave. He in danger. Enemies of state. He stay, he die. And you injured. Dying. Needed his help." The Captain looked thoughtfully towards the thing they called a crow's nest, where Yi Xiao sat, pretending to 'cultivate' himself. The damned fool couldn't even find a better lie to explain his cowardice. The mystic mumbo jumbo of the mountain sages was mere nonsense.

Everything Burton was telling her they'd told her before. Some of it might even be true. Gan Han's mother had said the young warrior resembled the Prince greatly. She'd even heard rumors that Yi Xiao was really the Prince's twin brother. He was born in the same place on the same day, after all. A twin to the Emperor's heir could only bring trouble to everyone around him.

"Stupid man," she muttered. "All he has to do is admit the truth and fight me."

"He fight you now, you die. Like Colonel Tsang."

"Who?"

"You not know who you fight, back Shanghai?" Burton shook his head at her ignorance. "Man who hurt you. He kill him. Still upset about."

The stupid man's lack of a spine was hardly Gan Han's problem. She waved off the implied criticism. "Why do you care, anyway? Don't you have something to be doing? A leak to stop? A sail to mend?"

"Could show you how," the Captain offered. "Would be something to do."

"I'd rather swim home." Noticing a faint dot on the horizon, she added, "Or you could find me a boat at that island up ahead." Not that she would have left. She couldn't go home until she'd defeated that idiot Yi Xiao.

"Island?" Captain Burton spun around, staring in the direction she'd indicated. Then, shouting something in English, he ran back to the mast, clambering up like the monkey he was.

Disinterested in whatever it was that'd upset the Captain, Gan Han sat back and sipped her tea, trying to think of some way she could get her desperately needed exercise again.

OOO

Captain Burton's sudden appearance in the crow's nest barely drew Yi Xiao's attention. He was having more trouble than usual calming his mind. It wasn't his destination bothering him, nor the reason for it. He'd already accepted the necessity and come to terms with it.

What he hadn't come to terms with was his own nature. He could lie to everyone else; tell them he was a man of peace, a follower of the *Dao*, seeking a balanced state of being. But he knew in his heart that his deep desire for those things was at odds with his love of danger and trouble. He'd liked fighting Colonel Tsang and had welcomed the excuse of Gan Han's condition to kill the man. Even now, several weeks after the fight, the memory of his blade sliding smoothly into Tsang's heart sang through his thoughts.

It sat ill with him, a bitter knowledge that the thing he'd tried so hard to erase from his heart simply would not leave him. How many would have to die before he gained control of his wolfish love of killing? "Master says, the heart feels as it must, but the brain and body need not follow."

"What the hell are you talking about? I said, why didn't you tell me about that island out there!?"

The Captain's demand finally got Yi Xiao's attention and he raised his eyes to the man. "Oh, that? It's been there for a little while now."

"And you didn't think to tell me?" Burton looked ready to shake him. "Damnit man...."

Standing, Yi Xiao peered at the faint dark mound in the distance. "Well, you said to watch for sails and ships, not islands."

"That's because there is no island out here!" Burton flung his hand at the sea in a broad gesture. Yi Xiao evaded easily, still eying the thing in the distance. "None!"

"Now that's just foolishness. It's quite obviously there...." Yi Xiao's answer trailed off as he took in Burton's meaning. "Oh. You mean it isn't on any of the charts?"

With an exasperated snort, Burton told him, "No. No, it is not. Which means we're off course! But how can we be off course? I checked it just an hour ago."

There was no pretending Yi Xiao understood the intricacies of naval navigation. "Could it be something other than an island? Some debris?"

Burton was already peering through his telescope so Yi Xiao waited and watched. Something moved at the edge of the horizon, a faint darkness rising above the shadowy mound. "Is that a ship?" he asked, pointing off to the side. If it was, it was in trouble, leaning sideways in the water.

"It is, damnit." Burton leaned over the edge of the crow's nest. "Ship ahoy. It's sinking! Twenty degrees starboard, now!"

It wasn't hard to guess what they were doing. Yi Xiao didn't know much about sea travel but it made sense that ships finding others in trouble would go to help. The one question he had was, "What about that island?"

"It looks a bit like a volcano, but I couldn't see any lava," Burton told him, keeping watch. "Don't know what's going on with it, but I'd bet my last dollar it has something to do with why that ship's in trouble. Wouldn't be the first time a volcano popped up out of nowhere to ruin some poor crew's day."

The description seemed inadequate, but Yi Xiao didn't argue. The *Henrietta Marie* was getting closer, so he could see the other ship's state without a telescope. Masts broken, sails rent, railing shattered, things were probably worse below decks. There was someone clinging to the only remaining mast, waving their free arm wildly.

"All hands!" Captain Burton roared. "We have a rescue!"

ooo

Ordinarily Burton's shouting wouldn't have drawn Gan Han's interest. She didn't like the man and would have happily ignored him. The fact the ship immediately changed course made her sit up and take notice. She looked around and spotted an odd shoal of sand surrounding an island that appeared to be formed of pure mud. Off to the side was another ship, this one smaller and lighter than Captain Burton's. It was better armed, too, with light cannons sticking out from every port.

Gan Han realized they were coming to the other ship's rescue and wondered if it were wise. Burton could be sailing straight into a trap. Admittedly, the closer they got, the more obvious the ship's damaged state became. Yet even injured men could turn on those who came to help them.

If she'd liked anyone aboard ship, Gan Han might have suggested rescue was risky. As it was, she welcomed trouble, if only to work off some of her anger. She shifted her position so she could watch the other vessel, expecting problems at any moment.

Burton's crew was already assisting survivors to escape their ruined ship. It took some time and Gan Han became more and more certain she didn't like the looks of the other crew. Neither did Burton's men, she was pleased to note. At least they weren't fool enough to blindly trust seeming helplessness.

One man, a short westerner with greying blond hair and a bright gold canine tooth, searched out Burton. He was speaking in English, what little Gan Han understood barely making sense. She thought he was thanking the Captain and asking if Burton would allow him to bring a chest aboard. Burton seemed to agree and the two men returned to the damaged ship with more assistants.

"It seems we're due some company," Yi Xiao said behind Gan Han, startling her into striking out at him. As usual, he wormed out of the way before she could touch him, so all she did was brush a bit of dirt from his shoulder. "Now, don't be that way."

"Don't sneak up on me, Yi Xiao!"

"I'm just a wanderer."

"I refuse to call you anything of the sort."

"Pity. I'm certainly not going to be anything else." Yi Xiao leaned against the railing, watching as the men dragged a heavily padlocked chest onto Burton's deck. "I wonder what's in the box. Gold? Tea? I hope not opium."

Westerners were always selling opium in China, causing more trouble with a few pounds of the drug than any thief or rebel. Gan Han refused to comment on it, saying only, "Why don't you ask?"

"I think I will...," Yi Xiao started to say, then paused, cocking his ear towards the ship. "Did you hear that?"

"Hear what?"

"Listen first," Yi Xiao said with annoying patience. When she shrugged, he added, "Someone shouted."

Again Gan Han shrugged. "So?"

"So there's still someone aboard."

It hardly mattered to her. "Maybe he's too injured to help and they left him there. Why do you care?" She was startled to see his concern. She was about to reach out to stop him but he was already over the edge of the ship and swimming for the damaged vessel. Within seconds he'd disappeared into the hole in its side, while Gan Han shrieked his name.

Burton, who'd been busy discussing something with the other ship's captain, raised his head. When he realized what Yi Xiao had done, he sighed and once again crossed over, yelling something incoherent as he went. Gan Han followed close behind. She wasn't going to be left out of the fun any longer.

ooo

The wreckage made it easier for Yi Xiao to board the other ship; the *Southern Cross*, or so the nameplate said. Broken spars gave him something to grasp and climb and the gash in the ship's side gave him an entrance. Luckily the ship had listed the other way. She would have sunk already otherwise.

There was a sound somewhere in the darkness of the hold. Weaker than before, it was the same desperate cry Yi Xiao had heard earlier. Likely its owner had little time left. Possibly Yi Xiao was already too late. He slid into wreckage filled water, struggling through the mess and feeling his way with his bare feet. Accustomed to the sharpened rocks of Heng Shan's peaks, he found the effort strangely familiar.

Again someone called and Yi Xiao called back, "I hear you. I'm coming." He spoke in Chinese, then English, hoping his tone would calm the trapped victim even if they didn't understand him.

"Damnit, Yi Xiao. Do you have an ounce of sense in that head of yours?" Burton's voice came from the deck above, where the man was peering through one of the cracks.

"He can call you Yi Xiao. Why won't you let me?" Gan Han demanded through another crack.

Yi Xiao sighed. "Master says, if you cannot keep your balance when the

world is flailing, you have not found the *Dao*." Before either of his unde-
sired audience could respond, he added, "There's someone in here. Find a
rope and help me get them out."

Gan Han didn't move from her spot, contenting herself with insults to
Yi Xiao's personality, his appearance and his courage. When she started in
on his parents, however, he drew a line. "You may insult me as much and
as often as you like. Insult my family and you insult my ancestors. I think
you know what an offense that is."

Although she sneered, Gan Han went silent on the matter. He was in
no position to accuse her of offending the Emperor's ancestors, but she
seemed to realize she'd gone too far. "You're an idiot."

"So I have been told by those around me for most of my life," Yi Xiao
admitted. "Indeed, as far as I can tell, you may be right."

"Why risk your life for a foreigner who may be dying already?"

"Because he isn't dead yet." By this time Yi Xiao had found the trapped
victim, a big man with broad shoulders, impressive muscles and features
of such mixed ancestry no one could be sure what it consisted of. He was
naked, chained to the wall, and looked as if he'd been severely beaten recently. That he'd survived this long spoke of stamina and stubborn deter-
mination. "And life is important."

"Hah!"

Ignoring her response, Yi Xiao focused his thoughts and examined the
first chain, searching the metal for its weakest point. Then, drawing on his
qi, he shattered the link with a single blow. He turned to the other chain
and repeated the process.

Suddenly a rope dangled down, followed by Burton's voice. "Do you
need me to come help?"

"Best not. I'll tie the rope around his waist and you can pull him up.
Though you may need assistance, he looks heavy." Yi Xiao didn't mention
the chain. He'd have to explain how he removed it and Burton didn't want
to know more about Yi Xiao's skills than absolutely necessary.

"Right. Let me know when you're ready."

After a few deep breaths to recover himself, Yi Xiao tied a makeshift
harness. "Pull him up," he called.

As the Captain tugged and strained to pull their rescue up out of the
water, Yi Xiao saw the man's eyes were open, his stoic expression hiding
some strong emotion. Anger? Hate?

Or was it fear?

OOO

" ...HE'D BEEN SEVERLY BEATEN RECENTLY. "

When they dragged the last survivor of the wrecked ship over to Burton's deck, the other victims shifted uneasily. The one, the man Gan Han assumed was their Captain, said something to Burton in a worried sort of way. Whatever it was, it didn't please the American. He said something about sea law, in a tone so hard it was obvious he'd brook no argument.

Not that the other Captain didn't try. Gold tooth flashing as he tried to persuade Burton of something, he gestured broadly, voice getting a little deeper and a little angrier with every sentence. At last Burton put his foot down, ordering the rescued crew below decks. They went, but their expressions were worrisome. Trouble was brewing; it was only a matter of time.

"What was all that about?" Gan Han demanded, assisting Yi Xiao with the rescued man's injuries. Not out of sympathy but because she wanted to harangue Yi Xiao further. Having him trapped with his latest patient seemed the best time to do so.

"That man says our patient is an insane criminal being transported to Australia." Done cleaning the man's injuries, Yi Xiao opened the little bundle of tools he'd been carrying in his pack. A jar of ointment, a spool of fine silk, with a gold needle thrust into its top, scissors, a fine sharp blade and a candle. He threaded the needle, lit the candle and heated its tip. "He thinks we put everyone at risk, rescuing him."

The ship shuddered, reminding Gan Han of the strange island that'd been slowly rising from the ocean. "From the volcano?"

"I think they mean our patient."

The man lying between them didn't look like he could do much. Oh, he was huge, easily six-foot tall and solidly built. Awake and uninjured, he'd be a dangerous opponent. Right now, however, he was a mess. Cuts and bruises covered his body and his coarse black hair was partially torn from his scalp. He'd lost a fight already and was in no condition for another.

Yi Xiao set a hand to the man's face, about to pull the cut on his forehead together to sew the flap of skin shut. As he did so, a huge hand grabbed him by the throat. The other hand caught Gan Han's wrist, pulling her down towards its owner. "Sorcerer," the man growled in Chinese. "I'll kill you if you lay your spells on me."

Gan Han slid her hand free and punched the man's shoulder, striking the center of one of his larger cuts. "Touch me again, I slit your throat," she snapped in turn. She wasn't going to put up with another damned idiot making a fool of himself. Before he could grab her, she somersaulted backwards. Instead of landing on her feet as she ought to have, she stumbled and fell to the ground, sprawling.

"Enough," Yi Xiao said, prying the man's fingers from his throat. He was clearly exasperated with both of them. "Gan Han, you're in no condition for acrobatics. Sir, I'm not a sorcerer, nor am I using magic to heal you. Relieve your mind of that fear."

"I saw what you did back there." The man's voice was weak, as weak as Gan Han felt. "Sorcerer!"

"What I did was a basic application of *qi*. Anyone trained to channel their inner energies into a physical blow could do the same." Yi Xiao began sewing up his patient's injury, using his knee to hold the man down. At the same time he lectured, spouting the foolish nonsense so beloved of mountain mystics.

It wasn't so much that Gan Han didn't understand or believe in *qi*. But Yi Xiao's claims were far beyond anything any human could do. As for Gods and Immortals; they didn't exist. "I wish you'd stop deceiving yourself. What you're saying is impossible."

Her statement made Yi Xiao frown at her, the moment of distraction almost netting him a blow to the eye. "Stop that. I'm trying to help. Do you want something to drink? It might make you feel better." When their patient simply growled a curse, he sighed, shifting position so he was kneeling on the man's arms, trapping them. "Gan Han, you were using your *qi* to protect yourself from Colonel Tsang's black aura. How can you claim you don't believe?"

"That's different." From the looks of things, this wasn't going to end quickly if someone didn't hold their patient down. She moved to his head and held it steady while Yi Xiao worked. "*Qi* flows through the body. All I was doing was redirecting his poison. And don't you dare bite me, you horrid man."

Again Yi Xiao frowned; though this time he kept his attention on his work. "His dark aura, you mean. Don't squirm." The last was directed at their unwilling patient.

"I mean his poison. You don't really think it was his spirit attacking me, do you?"

"Will the two of you let me go?"

"When I'm finished." Yi Xiao stitched up the wound crossing the man's forehead. "I do think that," he admitted to Gan Han. "But if you don't, there isn't much point in arguing the matter."

"I don't need help!" The man tried to kick his way out of Yi Xiao's hold but the idiot would-be priest was ready for that. He sat down hard on his patient's chest, knocking the wind from him.

"Good. Because I don't believe that and I refuse to be convinced. Better if you just give up the whole thing and return to the blade." Gan Han spread some of the ointment Yi Xiao gave her on their patient's injuries, adding, "Although you won't have it long because I will defeat you."

"You can't beat me, with or without a weapon," Yi Xiao retorted, sewing up the last of their patient's worst gashes. "Just drop the subject, Gan Han. It isn't happening."

Gan Han refused to argue the point any longer. He was right about one thing. She couldn't beat him yet. Her body was still too exhausted from her injuries. But they had over a month of travel left before they reached San Diego. Plenty of time for her to recover and show him exactly what she was made of.

Given, of course, they weren't all murdered in their sleep by the homicidal madman Yi Xiao had seen fit to rescue.

The rest of the day was spent getting the *Henrietta Marie* as far from the strange island as possible. With the excitement of the rescue over, the peculiarity of the thing made everyone nervous. Even Yi Xiao, born and raised miles from the sea, could tell the island was about as wrong as an island could be. For one thing, the vast majority of its surface had no solid ground beneath it. Rather it consisted of oddly light particles of sand, floating atop the water around a central cone of gushing mud.

"I've never seen anything like it before," Burton told him as the island receded in the distance behind them. "We're just lucky it wasn't a real volcano. We'd be charred ash otherwise."

That much was obvious. Of course, if it had been a volcano, Yi Xiao liked to think they wouldn't have been fool enough to get as close to it as they had. "It doesn't seem to be rising very fast, though. Do you really think it's dangerous?" Admittedly, he did, but he didn't know enough to be sure.

"I don't think it's safe, that's what I think." Burton glanced downwards though he couldn't see the other danger on his mind. "Anymore than that fellow you insisted on saving is."

Yi Xiao wouldn't argue the point of whether or not he should have saved the man. Whatever he was, murderer, madman or innocent victim, he was a living being. "Master says, life is important. Save it where you can."

"Your master isn't here to have her throat slit if he breaks free of the brig and murders us all in our sleep!" Burton said plaintively. "He's huge. I don't have the sort of chains needed to keep him under control."

"I don't know that we need any." Once the man—Hai Chan—had been patched up and given food and drink he'd sulkily cooperated with Yi Xiao. If he was to be believed, the *Southern Cross* was his own ship and Kramer and his men pirates who'd killed his crew. Hai Chan would've been next if that island hadn't erupted at exactly the wrong moment. The only reason Burton hadn't thrown them all in the brig was because he didn't have space. He'd decided to pretend Kramer was honest and keep close watch on him and his men.

"Do you believe he'll stay put?"

"His captors injured him badly. He's too weak to break free." Besides, Yi Xiao had given Hai Chan a dose of sleeping drug. Not from distrust, but because he—like Gan Han—had no sense when it came to rest.

Burton frowned at Yi Xiao curiously. "You're sure his injuries weren't from the accident?"

Some of the bruises and cuts certainly were, yet Yi Xiao, experienced in such matters from a lifetime in the martial world, recognized knife cuts when he saw them. The prisoner had been slashed repeatedly and beaten within an inch of his life. He said as much, adding, "It's a tribute to his stamina that he survived. Perhaps that's why they chained him; he frightened them so much they didn't dare risk his recovering enough to attack them."

That obviously didn't make Burton feel better. "It still doesn't prove he's innocent. He's dangerous, whatever the truth is." When Yi Xiao didn't answer, the Captain sighed. "I don't like casual killing, either, and I know you want to be done with that. We'll just have to keep an eye on him and the others."

"Wise choice." Years of training in the martial world had honed Yi Xiao's senses. If he was right, and his sense of danger was seldom wrong, then someone in their band of survivors was looking on the crew with killing intent.

The only question was, would they act on it?

○○○

Having more men aboard ship meant Gan Han had even less room for exercise than before. Worse, these newcomers—ill-mannered boors each and every one—spent their days idling around on deck, ogling her and getting in the way. The only times they weren't a constant bother, mispronouncing her name and pretending to court her, was from late at night to mid-morning, when they all lazed about in their bunks.

The only time the ship was truly quiet was in the early morning hours. Then all Gan Han could hear from her tiny room was the creaking of the ship's timbers, the flapping of its sails and the mutters of those few crewmen keeping watch. She knew Yi Xiao was up. The idiot practiced the style he claimed his master taught him in the early morning. Gan Han had watched him once, prancing around on deck wearing nothing but a pair of loose trousers as he waved a pair of scarves around. He'd looked a fool.

It finally occurred to Gan Han that she'd have the deck to herself if she rose earlier than Yi Xiao. It took several days of trying, but finally—about a week after they'd rescued the crew of the *Southern Cross*—she found the deck empty of everyone but the lookout. The skinny little boy was too shy to argue with her, leaving her to practice to her heart's content. As long as she finished before Yi Xiao came on deck, she could hide her techniques and her slowly recovered strength.

Over two weeks after the rescue, Gan Han came on deck for her usual practice and was surprised to find the young lookout missing. She'd have ignored the peculiarity if not for the fact that he was a responsible boy. He wouldn't have left his post unattended without good reason.

Lit by a few lanterns and no moonlight, the shadowy deck made her feel oddly nervous. The silence, broken only by the wind and lapping waves, seemed ominous. Was she imagining it? Or did she sense the faintest edge of a killing intent, somewhere near? If so, it wasn't aimed at her.

Gan Han walked around the deck and peered through the shadows. All she could see were the things she'd become accustomed to. A box here, a pile of carefully coiled rope there, a sleeping deckhand in a corner. With all the extra men aboard ship, everyone had had to find some place to bunk and this one had chosen an out of the way spot near the railing.

Yet there was something wrong about the figure. Gan Han stopped. Listened. Moved slowly and quietly closer. Even the quietest sleeper made some noise and this man was utterly still. It only took a moment to realize he was dead, his throat slit from ear to ear.

A hand slid around Gan Han's mouth and a stranger whispered something in a barbaric language. She didn't need to understand the words to know the intent. She was to remain still and make no sound. Otherwise the pinprick against her throat would turn into something worse.

The man—one of the *Southern Cross's* crew—dragged her off to the side. Some of his fellows were moving in the shadows, silent and cautious as they took up their positions. No doubt they were preparing to take over the ship and under some circumstances; Gan Han might not have cared who did what to whom. This time her own life was at stake.

Yi Xiao had yet to return Gan Han's sword to her, but that didn't make her helpless. Death Flower techniques incorporated both blade and weighted sleeve fighting. Besides, no true martial artist could depend entirely on having their chosen weapon to hand. She could attack whenever she chose, biding her time so as to make it count.

Several members of the *Southern Cross's* crew gathered together near the man holding Gan Han captive. One said something softly, tone faintly mocking as he eyed her. She didn't need to understand their foreign babble to guess at what they'd said, nor what they'd suggested for her. Or for the lookout another man had captured.

Gan Han's captor chuckled, tightening his grip in an ugly mockery of an embrace. Somehow, she managed not to react, not even to allow her expression to show her anger. She wasn't afraid of them. There were only four untrained fighters. Even without her sword she was sure she could handle them. She just needed the right moment.

Someone pushed open the hatch leading to the lower deck and shoved a mostly unconscious Hai Chan through. A voice spoke from beneath, saying something about being ready to start now. It was rare for Gan Han to regret her limited English. The foreign devils' babble was unseemly and unpleasant but knowing what her captors were up to would have been useful. No doubt they planned on taking over the *Henrietta Marie*. She just didn't know how.

One of the men chuckled and kicked Hai Chan in the side. Still groggy from Yi Xiao's medicines, he didn't react. A slightly harder kick barely elicited an "oof" and still failed to rouse him. Gan Han didn't bother trying to stop their abuse. Hai Chan wasn't her responsibility after all.

Another man spoke, suggesting it didn't matter. He said more, Hai Chan and Captain Burton's names, together with the word for death. Gan Han guessed the plan. They meant to make it look as if Hai Chan had broken free and murdered the Captain. Likely they'd kill him as well, so he couldn't protest his innocence.

One of the foreigners headed towards the door to Captain Burton's cabin, only to be interrupted by Hai Chan's gruff voice, his tone combining anger and triumph. "Bastards! You'll pay for what you've done!" He rolled sideways, out of the men's reach, and came to his feet.

At the same time one of the conspirators went flying, flung there by a strike between the shoulders. Yi Xiao called out, "Now, Gan Han!"

Recognizing her cue and appreciating the idiot warrior's trust in her good sense, Gan Han slammed her elbow into her captor's sternum, twisting just enough to keep his blade from slicing her throat open. Freed of his grip, she smashed her weighted sleeve into the man's temple. Bone shattered and he went down in a heap.

Hai Chan was knocking heads together. At the same time, Yi Xiao danced with the last pair of foreigners. At least, that was the only way Gan Han could describe his fighting technique. Slippery as a snake, he shifted and twisted, catching hold of wrists and sliding his feet between his opponents', tripping them. It was a cowardly style, unseemly for a man as skilled with the blade as he.

Gan Han saw another pair of foreigners climb out from a grate towards the bow of the ship. Rather than watch Yi Xiao make a fool of himself, she paused to snatch the stiletto from the man she'd killed, then rushed at the pair. The weapon wasn't her favorite choice, but it was all she had.

Dodging the first man, she sliced the tip of her blade across the other's cheek. As blood flowed and he shouted, she swung her long weighted sleeve. It wrapped itself around the man's wrist and she used it to spin him around, tangling him in the fabric's length.

The other man grabbed for her, but she evaded him easily, blocking his grasp with her blade. He screamed, blood spurting from his palm as her weapon cut deep. She was about to bury the blade in his chest when a loud bang startled her into turning.

The captain of the *Southern Cross* stood over Hai Chan with a huge cutlass in one hand and a pistol in the other. Yi Xiao, cowardly as ever, was backing away. Annoyed, Gan Han snapped, "Damn you, do your duty!"

"My duty doesn't include getting shot," Yi Xiao countered. "Especially with a magically enhanced weapon."

There being no such thing as magic, Gan Han disregarded the argument. "If you won't, I will." She stabbed her opponent, skewering him through the heart before he had a chance to shriek. She was about to go after the foreigner when Hai Chan flipped back to his feet and barred her path with an overly muscled arm.

"Get out of my way," Gan Han ordered.

"You're not up to it, little girl," Hai Chan growled. "The damned bastard's spell's more than I could handle, much less you." His chest and shoulder were blackened and charred as if someone had taken a torch and pressed it to his bare flesh. Another man would have been screaming in agony, but they'd already established that Hai Chan had immense reserves against pain.

"You're not a warrior of the Death Flowers." The very fact that this idiot sailor thought she wasn't his equal was an insult. "I'm more than a match for any so-called sorcerer."

Yi Xiao caught her wrist and pulled her back. "No. He's right. You were already hurt on my behalf. No need to repeat the experience."

This seemed a chance to force her rival into returning to his true and proper path. "In that case, get your sabre and fight him. Prove you're my better."

"I don't need a blade to prove myself." Yi Xiao's expression shifted, as if the boast were something to be ashamed of. "Just get back. We'll find a way to get rid of him."

"If you're so good you can fight that man without your sabre and win, I'll accept you've chosen the right path for yourself," Gan Han told him, knowing full well she couldn't keep her promise. "Show me your skill, Yi Xiao. Prove the value of what the Storm Hermit has taught you."

○○○

The bargain was one Yi Xiao yearned to avoid. Not because he doubted his skill against Captain Kramer's sorcery. The Westerner's magic, and magic it certainly was, required a focus to work. It also required time to use; enough time that Yi Xiao was fairly sure he could evade it. As for taking the man down without killing? Kramer might be a sorcerer, but he'd no skill in the martial arts. His movements proved that much.

No. It was the fact that Yi Xiao was forced to bargain at all that bothered him. He'd been unsuccessful in persuading Gan Han that he wasn't the man she'd been hunting for. Unsuccessful in persuading the girl that there was no need for the two of them to fight. Unsuccessful in persuading her that he'd left the martial world. A challenge like this risked rousing his love of fighting and bloodshed and he wanted so desperately to be done with all that.

Yet still, he seemed to have no choice but to fight. "Give me your sleeves," he ordered Gan Han. He'd left his own scarves with his things below, where he'd been guarding Hai Chan. When she glared at him, about to refuse, he pointed out, "You want me to show you my skill. I don't have to have them, but they'd be useful."

With a dour expression, Gan Han sliced her sleeves from her outer robe. "You'll replace them, you know." It wasn't a request.

"I will." Yi Xiao turned his attention back to Kramer, whose only reason for giving them time to prepare was that it gave him time as well. The man had been infusing his magic in bullet after bullet while they'd talked, so that now he had a dozen of the things.

Quick analysis told Yi Xiao why the enemy captain didn't carry his ensorcelled bullets around with him, ready for any eventuality. Why, too, the captain didn't give his spell to anyone else. It required its creator to maintain it. Which, in turn, meant Kramer couldn't be as strong as he wanted them to believe.

Oh, the spell was powerful. It'd injured Hai Chan badly after all. It wasn't, however, the work of a master sorcerer. The man had learned to imbue his spells into the bullets but had yet to learn to embed the magic the spell needed to operate. Any sorcerer worth their spells could do that much, yet Kramer clutched the bullets in his spare hand, obviously using his physical contact to maintain the magic.

So the first thing to do was to disarm his enemy of as many of his little toys as possible. Yi Xiao hefted Gan Han's sleeves, telling his allies, "Back up. Weighted, these things are deadly." Gan Han knew that already. She'd killed her captor with one blow, after all. Yet she didn't complain at Yi Xiao's including her in the order. She was too busy watching him closely, trying to understand what he was doing.

Kramer sneered. "You'll have to get to me first, Chinaman."

"True." Yi Xiao flipped sideways, a cartwheel that needed no hands to help him spin. When he landed, he let loose with one of Gan Han's sleeves, letting it brush his enemy's robe. Deliberately, he cursed, as if the blow had been intended to do much more and much worse.

The enemy captain loaded the first of his many bullets into his weapon, aiming it for Yi Xiao's heart, then fired at Gan Han instead. It burst into flame as it passed, forcing Yi Xiao to use one of the girl's sleeves to block it. Immediately the fabric caught fire, or tried to. Yi Xiao let his *qi* flow through the cloth, washing away the flames before they did more than sear it.

Kramer's bullets were far faster than anything Yi Xiao had dealt with so far. If he weren't using his *qi* to redirect any energy flung his way, he would have taken the next shot straight to the chest. There were those who claimed they could harden their skin against bullets but Yi Xiao wasn't one of them. Even if he became a true master of the Wind and Rain style he'd never manage such a feat.

Again Kramer loaded his weapon and again Yi Xiao redirected the shot with his *qi*. Behind him, Gan Han was yelling, telling him to stop prancing around like a street actor. Hai Chan remained silent, much to Yi Xiao's relief. Already they'd attracted attention as the rest of the crew, finally realizing there was trouble, began gathering on deck. Now he'd have to worry about them as well as himself.

The noise drew Captain Burton out, but all he said was, "Don't make a mess on my ship. A bigger mess, that is." He must have noticed Gan Han and Hai Chan's victims, their blood seeping into the deck behind Yi Xiao. Or maybe it was the burn marks from Kramer's magic. Yi Xiao ignored the complaint, dodging another bullet, this one coming within inches of his face as he arched backwards to evade it.

"This is a fight, not a dance," Gan Han snapped. "Do something useful. Preferably fatal."

It seemed Yi Xiao was in the minority. Gan Han, Hai Chan, the *Henrietta Marie's* crew, even Captain Burton, all seemed entirely agreeable with the idea of his killing Kramer. The fact that killing was a thing Yi Xiao wanted to be done with didn't matter to them in the slightest. Knowing his argument would fall on deaf ears, he countered, "I am a Priest of the Wind and Rain. Not a blood-thirsty murderer."

"Doesn't matter anyway. You're the one going to die." Kramer's knowledge of Chinese was unexpected but Yi Xiao supposed any man who sailed the Pacific was going to pick up at least a little of the local languages. "You and everyone else aboard this ship."

Burton asked reasonably. "How are you going kill us all? You're alone now."

"The hell I am."

"The hell you aren't. I knew you were up to something. My men were just waiting for yours to attack. Those they haven't killed already are all tied up down in the bilge. "

Yi Xiao used the man's moment of distraction to roll right in front of him, striking his gut as hard as he could. The *qi* enhanced blow knocked Kramer off his feet. Unfortunately, that wasn't enough to stop him. He rose unsteadily, catching hold of a gaff. It glowed under his touch and Hai Chan called out a warning. "Don't let him hit you."

That much was obvious. Apparently Kramer could imbue more than bullets with his magic. Yi Xiao had no doubts about the danger. He flipped backwards to avoid the weapon, using Gan Han's sleeves to distract his enemy. The man used the gaff, catching Yi Xiao's weapon and tangling it in the hook. His magic flowed into the sleeve and this time there was too much for Yi Xiao to block with his *qi*. The sleeve caught fire and burned away.

Kramer thrust his gaff at Yi Xiao again. Knowing better than to allow it, Yi Xiao raced at him and, instead of simply striking with his remaining sleeve, leapt into the air, somersaulting over the man and slamming the weight into the back of his head. Kramer fell forward and lay, half-stunned, on the blood-stained deck.

Relieved, thinking Kramer was done, Yi Xiao relaxed, about to turn to Captain Burton and tell him to put the man in the brig. Except Gan Han cried out, "What's happening to him?" For the first time she actually sounded scared.

Yi Xiao's opponent seemed to be glowing. He spread his hands flat, the same glow seeping from his entire body and into the deck. A stain of reddish gold, the color of his magic, spread outwards. "I don't like the look of that," Burton murmured.

"Get back. All of you." Yi Xiao's warning didn't come fast enough. One of Burton's men, curious and unfortunately foolhardy, poked the stain with his dagger. Immediately the glow enveloped the blade and went straight up the man's hand and arm. Within seconds he was a glowing, screaming, struggling thing, trying to break free of whatever it was Kramer had created.

Yi Xiao moved quickly. He'd neither choice or time. He dropped into water summoning stance, shouting, "Get out of the way!" Then he drew on his inner power, gathering it together as he stepped in the slow, stately, pattern of the Mountain Dragon's Dance. His *qi* flowed along with him, flaring brilliantly in a profligate and dangerous use of power. He'd learned the pattern but he'd hardly come close to mastering it. If he got one thing wrong, failed his concentration, he'd be transformed and lost forever.

The power flowed through him, water and wind combining to form a cloud of chill vapor, tiny daggers of ice spinning around him in a whirlwind. It flowed across the deck, danced along with him, singing its ancient and wordless song. Someone screamed Yi Xiao's name but he ignored their call. He had to wash that stain of magic from this ship before it consumed it entirely.

Its heat and his swirling fog struck each other. Ice blades shattered and melted, flames smoked and faded. If Kramer had been a stronger or better sorcerer, Yi Xiao's *qi* storm could never have defeated him. As it was, it took just about all Yi Xiao had to force the burning magic—including its creator—to the center of his power. Then, knowing he was ending a life again, and grieving for it, he sent the whole seething mess overboard, to explode in the depths of the ocean.

As he let his *qi* fade, Yi Xiao fell to his knees. Burton was there a moment later, keeping him from landing on his face. Then Gan Han approached. "Is that proof enough?" he asked, but was too close to unconsciousness to comprehend her answer.

OOO

It wasn't possible. It couldn't be possible. Yet Gan Han couldn't deny what she's seen. "What was that?" she whispered, barely able to breathe.

"Sorcery, as I told you," grumbled Hai Chan. "What else?"

Yi Xiao had been just as insistent that he wasn't a sorcerer. Nor was it a point worth arguing. Whatever power it was the young noble had displayed, it wasn't natural. Was this how he'd become so skilled at the blade? It'd make Gan Han's life easier; after all, she could hardly be expected to outmatch a man whose talent was a mere cheat.

Still, easier though the revelation might be, she sensed she'd be wrong to assume it. The power Yi Xiao had wielded had nothing to do with his blade-work. No technique she could think of involved the strange leaps, spins and bounds the young man made use of. She'd seen his grandmother at work once, years ago. Wolf Fang style was rapid and direct, relying mostly on speed and offense. The only thing the Storm Hermit of Heng Shan's technique shared with the White Wolf Blade was incredible speed and agility.

"Hey! You help him. I have a ship to care for." Captain Burton again, his abysmal Chinese an affront to any native speaker. Gan Han swallowed her criticism. The idiot wasn't worth her time. Besides, he was right that Yi Xiao needed help and she doubted the man had a clue how to manage it.

Hai Chan called out to the Captain, "I'm no doctor. I'll help you. I know ships better than healing."

The foreign devil didn't look as if he liked the idea. Still, he obviously needed an extra hand. The fight with Kramer and his men had killed or incapacitated several of his men. Raised aboard her family's junk, Gan Han knew the *Henrietta Marie* didn't have many extra crewmen. Captain Burton would need as many hands as he could get.

As the others went to work getting the ship back in order and back on course, Gan Han dragged Yi Xiao's barely cooperating body to her berth. There wasn't a mark on him and aside from looking drawn and exhausted, he seemed unharmed. She corrected herself. Half-conscious though he was, there was a twist to his brows suggesting deep unhappiness. "What is it?"

His eyes fluttered. Opened briefly. "Master says, the true *Dao* makes killing unnecessary. I fail. Over and over I fail her. Over and over I fail myself."

Gan Han felt a surge of rage and jealousy towards the Hermit of Heng Shan. How had the woman managed to twist Yi Xiao so far out of his true and proper path as a weapons master? How had she managed to transform the deadliest killer the martial world had ever known to this... this... ineffectual crybaby?

"You don't have to find that stupid *Dao*."

"I want to find that stupid *Dao*," Yi Xiao said firmly, opening his eyes again and looking at her with strange and oddly powerful calm. "And if I fail now, I keep trying. I will not fight you, Gan Han. Not to prove a thing I no longer need."

Almost at a loss for words, all Gan Han managed was, "I'll follow you until you do."

"You're welcome to try." Yi Xiao turned his back to her. "But first you'll have to find my path."

Chapter 3: Wood –
Gathering Together with Limitations

The rest of the journey to San Diego was relatively uneventful by Hai Chan's standards. He'd been a sailor all his life and was accustomed to the little excitements of ocean life. Being boarded by pirates had been about the worst and he still felt he could have handled the bastards if their Captain hadn't been a sorcerer. The storms and long windless days, however, were as normal as the constant squabbles between dozens of strong personalities crowded together in close quarters. He gladly left the arguments to Burton.

Besides, Hai Chan had his own argument with Yi Xiao to pursue.

" I WANT TO FIND THAT STUPID *DAO.* "

Unlike that silly chit, Gan Han, he didn't need or want to fight the man. He knew what the martial world was, but he'd never been interested in joining it, any more than he wanted anything to do with sorcery. Making Yi Xiao admit the truth of what he did, however, would have been eminently satisfying.

Yi Xiao was a stubborn creature, though, and Hai Chan didn't know enough about sorcery to prove him wrong. Yet he couldn't believe the thing the priest called *qi* wasn't magic, no matter how often Yi Xiao patiently explained the difference. So what if *qi* was an internal power, born of the wielder's spiritual energy? It was still a power that could be directed beyond flesh to act on the world.

At least Gan Han no longer pretended there was no such thing as magic. Kramer's sorcery had proved her wrong on that count. She didn't understand it any better than Hai Chan but at least she wasn't sneering at his childish belief in such things. She still sneered at his uneducated, uncomplicated and unconcerned ways, while he called her what she was; a self-absorbed, childish, and bloodthirsty little girl. The martial world seemed rife with people like her.

It made Hai Chan wonder how Yi Xiao, sweet-tempered and strangely imperturbable as he was, had avoided becoming like Gan Han. Any descendent of the Qing emperors, particularly one belonging to a powerful family in the martial world ought to have grown up knowing their place and power. Kindness, a desire to do no harm, those weren't things Hai Chan associated with men like Yi Xiao. He, himself, had been forced to flee his hometown because the local clans had started a war with each other.

Still, Yi Xiao was oddly likable, aside from his insistence that his magic was nothing of the sort. He was a facile conversationalist and amusing to watch, especially when he teased Gan Han. It made Hai Chan's plans for his own future easier to decide. "When we reach port I will go with you to San Francisco."

The young priest was puzzled. "I've no objection, but why? You're a sailor; why not remain aboard the *Henrietta Marie*? Captain Burton seems to have found some use for you."

Staying with Captain Burton would be profitable, certainly. The westerner might be annoyingly overconfident in some matters but he knew his job and he did it well. Still, "I was captain of my own ship. I intend to be again." At Yi Xiao's confused expression, he added, "You don't know how things are in California right now?"

"I don't," Yi Xiao admitted. "Enlighten me?"

"You've at least heard they found gold last year, somewhere near a place called Sutter's Mill?"

"I've been training on Heng Shan for the last two years," Yi Xiao pointed out.

The mountain range of Heng Shan was far enough inland that news from a barbaric place like America wouldn't reach that far. Moreover, if Yi Xiao's stories about his training were to be believed, a disciple of any mountain priest would have little to no contact with the outside world.

"Well, they did. So much gold, in fact, that miners and prospectors have been pouring into California ever since. It's gotten to the point that captains don't dare land in San Francisco. Their crews desert to go hunting for gold and their ships sit in dock, empty and useless."

Yi Xiao worked out Hai Chan's intentions quickly. "So you plan on absconding with an abandoned ship? How will you get a crew, if they're all mining for gold?"

"I'll find a way." It wasn't as easy to make one's fortune as gold-hungry prospectors thought. By now there'd be disaffected and disappointed would-be miners, beginning to realize just how futile their search really was. Hai Chan would find them and somehow persuade them aboard ship, then sail as far from San Francisco's golden trap as possible. He'd show them they'd profit more trading and hauling goods around the Pacific. There was no reason, no reason at all, why Americans and Englishmen should be the only ones to gain from the western appetite for tea and other Chinese goods.

All without trading a single ounce of opium.

ooo

Yi Xiao's return to land proved amusingly awkward. As he walked down the gangplank onto the relatively steady surface of San Diego's dock, he nearly fell into the water. He stumbled over his own feet before managing to steady himself by catching hold of a post and clinging tight. He grinned broadly at his own clumsiness. "I could do with a bath, but not that way."

"You are embarrassing," Gan Han grumbled. Her glare would have cut right through him if her sword had been involved.

"You were raised aboard your family's junk," Yi Xiao pointed out, chuckling as he recovered himself. "You knew to expect this. I didn't."

"Idiot," she muttered under her breath.

Ignoring the girl's complaints, Yi Xiao turned his attention to the broadly grinning Captain Burton. "I believe we part ways now."

"I'm afraid so. It's been interesting, traveling with you, but...."

"Excuse me! Sir? Excuse me?" The Captain broke off as a tall, rangy, black-haired westerner hurried towards him with an anxious and irritated expression. He was overdressed for the warm weather and his thick wool shirt was soaked in sweat. There were two men behind him, equally over-dressed and sweaty.

Burton frowned. "Can I help you?"

"Sir, are you the captain of this fine vessel?" The westerner's accent was one Yi Xiao didn't recognize. There was a lilt to it, or a drawl, of a sort he'd never heard before. It sounded American, but not the same as Burton's.

"I am."

"Thank God you've come. I am Reverend Josiah Burns. I, and my companions, ten men in all, would travel with you to San Francisco. We have...."

Burton stopped the man from continuing. "Sir, I appreciate your desire, but the *Henrietta Marie* is headed to Panama after this. I have cargo promised to be there within the month and no time for any detours."

Burns tried to argue. "But we've been stranded here for two weeks!" He gestured north. "The fishing boat we hired in Panama abandoned us here. We've been hoping to find someone, anyone, to take us the rest of the way to San Francisco."

"Didn't you come around the Horn? You should have stayed with your ship."

Burns waved off the question. "We came to Panama through the Gulf and hiked across the isthmus." An irritated expression crossed his face as he added, "And it weren't no easy trip, I can tell you that."

Yi Xiao visualized the map and wondered why Burns was so annoyed. It was just around fifty miles across the isthmus. It wouldn't take much more than a week to make the trip, even through jungle. He didn't ask, contenting himself with listening and, he hoped, learning.

"I quite understand," Burton commiserated. "I've traveled that way once or twice myself. Jungle, not much trail to speak of and the mosquitoes. I hope you brought plenty of quinine."

"We did, and good thing, too. One youngster was so sick he nearly died." Burns shrugged off the concern, adding, "But you understand our frustration?"

Burton agreed. "I do. I'm guessing your plan was to avoid Cape Horn and spend less time asea?" he asked curiously and when Burns agreed, added, "What I don't understand is why you didn't hire a proper ship in Panama to take you all the way to San Francisco. Fishermen have better things to do with their time than ferry people several thousand miles from home."

With an angry snort, Burns explained, "There aren't any ships coming back from San Francisco. Word is as soon as they get there, their crews desert and leave their ships stranded."

"I see." Burton spread his hands helplessly, "You have my deepest sympathies but I can't help you. I've given my word."

Anger flashed across the man's face. "I and my companions are to starve here, then?"

Yi Xiao doubted they'd starve. San Diego looked to be a busy port, with plenty of jobs for able and willing men.

"I don't suggest that. You could go by land. El Camino Real is...."

"That so-called trail the Mexicans left us? Are you mad? It's over five hundred miles to San Francisco by land. And we have our gear and food to carry as well!"

Worried by the man's insistence and suspicious of the way they stared longingly at the *Henrietta Marie*, Yi Xiao rose to his feet, nearly overbalancing. Burton caught his arm, muttering, "This isn't the time for your circus act."

"I'm not even sure what that is," Yi Xiao countered, speaking in Chinese. "Never mind that. May I make a suggestion?"

Burns glared at the interruption, while Burton, guessing Yi Xiao didn't want what he said to be understood, responded in the same language. "What is?"

"They look desperate. They may try to take what is not given."

Burton considered that. "I won't disagree. What suggest?"

"They hired a fisherman to get them this far. Tell them to do so again. Even if they can't find someone willing to make the whole trip, they could hire fresh boats wherever they stop." Yi Xiao had been studying Burton's maps carefully, knowing he'd have to find his way north on his own. He'd considered doing the same thing himself, but he'd had quite enough of shipboard life. He yearned for the relative quiet of the road.

"What's that heathen Chinee servant of yours saying?" Burns demanded.

"He's not a servant. He's a passenger," Burton corrected. "He suggested you hire another fisherman. They might not get you all the way, but you could keep hiring boats until you're there."

The man scoffed. "What a waste of time and money!"

"Maybe, but otherwise you'll have to walk, or keep hoping to find a ship willing to risk its crew to the lure of the gold fields." Burton inclined his head politely, "And now, if you don't mind, I have business to settle. I'm sorry I can be of no further use to you."

"But...."

"Good day, sir. I wish you luck in finding your way." Burton turned his attention back to his own business, ignoring the way Burns' mouth worked. Once again speaking in Chinese, he told Gan Han, "As soon as my work done, will return you home. Wait here."

Without a word, Gan Han walked back aboard ship, ignoring Yi Xiao's cheerful farewell. Once she was out of sight, Burton ordered his second-mate to pull up the gangplank. "No one boards without my permission, no matter who it is nor how important."

"Understood sir."

"Yi Xiao, Hai Chan. Not know if we meet again, but if do, hope to find you well. Safe journey, you both."

Recognizing it was high time they were on their way, Yi Xiao headed into town. He didn't mind walking to San Francisco, but Hai Chan hadn't liked the idea when he'd proposed it earlier. They'd have to find horses and guidance. The Road of the King was supposed to be well-marked, but he knew little of local customs. He hoped to find someone to advise them.

ooo

The trouble with Yi Xiao was he kept so much of his thoughts to himself. Hai Chan didn't even know why the man was headed to San Francisco. Nor did asking help. Yi Xiao's only answer was, "Because I am a filial grandson."

By this time they were halfway through a pleasant little town of odd buildings built of wood and clay. Most were colored some light shade, with attractively painted windows and doors. All were strange to Hai Chan's eyes. There wasn't a single properly curved roof in sight. Indeed, some of the buildings didn't have true roofs at all, just flat tops with bars of wood sticking out.

Yi Xiao gawked unabashedly, ambling down the street with the loose limbed movement of one accustomed to long, slow walks. It was a difficult speed for Hai Chan. He was taller than Yi Xiao by several inches and had to adjust his steps to match his companion's. The priest could move quickly when he wanted, but this wasn't one of those times.

"Do you have the slightest idea what you're looking for?"

"A little, yes. Burton told me where the market was. We may not find horses or a guide there, but perhaps I can get someone to change my silver to something more useful." Yi Xiao paused to evade a group of children whose appearance reminded Hai Chan of Southern Chinese. They ran around Yi Xiao, screaming with laughter, especially when he pretended to trip and fall over them, performing a little dance to evade their rapid movements.

"I can see why that silly girl of yours gets so mad at you. You're a buffoon." Everything Yi Xiao did was surely an affront to Gan Han's dignity.

"She isn't my girl, you realize?"

"She seems to think so."

Yi Xiao snorted, "Not really. She's looking for her mother's approval, not a man's love." He looked thoughtful, adding, "I'm not the sort she'd want, anyway."

Thinking about it, Hai Chan supposed he might be right. He didn't need to ask why Yi Xiao behaved so oddly. The young man's nonsense kept people at a distance. There was a hidden part of his personality he wished no one to approach too closely. Hai Chan had caught a glimpse of it, that day when Yi Xiao had slain Kramer. The man played at being kind and gentle, even humorous, but there was an underlying violence to him, a love of killing terrifying in its intensity.

"She seems to have given up on whatever she wanted from you, at least."

"Thank the Gods, yes." Yi Xiao wiped his forehead in an exaggerated way. "I don't need to spend the rest of my days avoiding her. And before you ask why I don't just let her beat me, she'd know if I pretended to fight."

Well, yes. It'd be the worst sort of insult to a warrior of the martial world. Gan Han's pride would never have put up with such an affront. Likely she'd force Yi Xiao to kill her, out of sheer obstinacy. "Just as well she's going home, then."

Yi Xiao agreed as they entered a large open area full of carts and people. It looked like any number of Chinese markets and though the produce was strange and unfamiliar, as were some of the scents, it felt like coming home. Hai Chan had spent a great deal of his childhood in markets like this and it made him feel more comfortable in this strange land, with so many unfamiliar sounds, smells and faces.

"Excuse me. Does anyone speak English here?" A westerner, one with an accent similar to the Reverend Burns', was trying to talk to the traders, most of who stared at him with blatant dislike. He was over-dressed the same way Burns had been, though unlike Burns he'd let his shirt hang open and wasn't bothering with a hat to cover his bright red hair. "Please?"

A boy, not much more than twelve, peered out from behind the man, his cropped red hair proving their relationship. He was looking around nervously, grey eyes wide and scared. "Pa," he said. "Maybe them two?" He pointed at Yi Xiao and Hai Chan. "They don't look like they're from around here."

The boy's father looked over at them. "Don't be silly, Jo. Them two are Chinamen. They don't speak no English, guaranteed."

If it'd been up to Hai Chan, he'd have pretended not to understand a word, to avoid getting caught up in some strangers' problems. Especially strangers obviously associated with that Burns fellow. Yi Xiao, on the other hand, was perfectly willing to stick his long nose into trouble. He cocked his head and smiled, saying, "I actually do speak English. And French. And German. And a bit of Russian. And several dialects of Chinese, of course, including Taiwanese, Manchurian, Cantonese and Mongolian. Though I'm afraid the last two are no better than my Russian. Still, I'm fluent enough to annoy people in a number of different languages. Which would you prefer?"

The boy was giggling by now, though there was still a scared look in his eyes that made Hai Chan think he and his father were in some trouble. His father was staring at Yi Xiao with an expression of disbelief, which made Hai Chan elbow his companion. "Don't be so damned ridiculous," he said in Chinese. "This isn't the time for your nonsense."

"There's always time for my nonsense," Yi Xiao argued, but stopped grinning like an idiot to add, once more in English, "If I can help you, I will. Though I'm not at all sure how useful I'll be. I'm just as much a stranger to this town as you."

The man said, quite slowly and more than a little hopefully, "You're a Christian convert?"

Though Hai Chan had learned his English from a missionary, he mostly felt impatient with their earnest and naïve attempts to persuade their students to follow their God. He considered saying as much but decided it might be better if he kept his knowledge of English to himself. Playing the ignorant fool could prove useful on occasion.

Yi Xiao, having proved his foolishness in other ways, went on as he'd begun. "I'm afraid not. But I assure you, I'm harmless. I can even be helpful, if you'll allow me. What sort of assistance do you need?"

"I don't even know who you are, much less if I can trust you. You talk pretty for a Chinaman, but...."

Yi Xiao bowed. "Thank you. My second mother says I talk too much, really. I also forget my manners. My name is Lang Yi Xiao, a wanderer headed for the city of San Francisco. This is Hai Chan, a sailor also headed for that city."

Hai Chan bowed, saying in Chinese, "Pleased to meet you."

The boy tugged at his father's coat and pulled him close, whispering something urgently. Hai Chan wasn't sure, but he thought the child said something about liking Yi Xiao. Giving in, the father said, "I'm Hal Kraft, Mr. Shee-ow. And I guess it's pretty obvious my kid here and I are headed to San Francisco too."

"Lang," Yi Xiao corrected. "In China, we use our family name first. Which, I suppose, means I should call myself Yi Xiao Lang here in America? Master says, when in Rome, do as the Romans do."

Kraft almost let himself be dragged along by the current of Yi Xiao's nonsense. "I suppose," he agreed. "But you said you can help? Do you know any Spanish? I'm trying to find someone to sell me a horse and a pack mule. I think some of these people know what I'm saying but they act like they can't understand a word."

"Regretfully, Spanish is not one of the languages I've learned. There are similarities with French, of course, but not enough. I was hoping to find an English speaker here as well, for the same reason."

"I... see." Kraft sounded disappointed but unsurprised.

It was obvious the grim-faced merchants understood more than they pretended. Something about the way they were studiously and obviously ignoring the outsiders' discussion made Hai Chan certain they were refusing to cooperate. He said as much to Yi Xiao.

"Interesting," Yi Xiao murmured and returned his attention to Kraft. "Is there a reason they might...." He trailed off, eyes on something further down the way. "Er... I think someone is looking for you."

Hai Chan followed Yi Xiao's gaze and saw Reverend Burns staring around the market, his fury obvious. The man spotted his fellow westerner and strode towards them rapidly, calling out Kraft's name as if he were a child who'd wandered from its keeper.

At the same time Jo dove below the nearest cart and scurried behind it. The old woman who owned it started to complain, then stopped suddenly when the boy put a pleading hand on her skirts. "*Bueno, bebita.* You hide here." Then, without another word, she sat down and closed her mouth tight, ignoring them all grimly.

"Hal, what in the name of heavenly glory are you doing, wandering around? Didn't I tell you it's dangerous?" Burns glanced briefly at Hai Chan and Yi Xiao. "Didn't I see you two... oh, wait. You don't speak a civilized tongue, why bother asking?"

To Hai Chan's surprise, Yi Xiao just smiled, the broad, friendly expression of a fool unaware he'd been insulted. Nor did he speak, leaving Kraft to say, "Jo was hungry for something asides from flatbread and dried meat. I thought I'd see if anyone here would sell me some fruit."

"Damnit, man, what did I say about letting me handle the natives? You're too trusting and they'll steal the shirt off your back, soon as look at you." Burns scanned the area. "Where is that... boy... of yours anyways?"

Kraft didn't miss a beat. "You said it was dangerous to wander around, so I left him back at the inn. Figured Joel and Cletis could keep an eye out on him for a little."

There was doubt in Reverend Burns' eyes but he didn't see Jo where the boy hid behind the old lady. He didn't argue, simply told Kraft. "Well I guess it's okay to get some fruit. Just make sure to wash it real good before we eat any. Can't tell where them as picked it have been. Come back to the inn as soon as you're done. That Yankee captain was being difficult and we gotta make plans like I said we would. Understand?"

"Right, sir. I understand you perfect."

"Good."

Burns didn't bother looking at Yi Xiao or Hai Chan again, just turned around and went the way he'd come. Hai Chan waited for him to be out of sight before saying, "You don't trust him much, do you, Mr. Kraft."

Yi Xiao leaned over to call Jo out from under the cart. "You especially don't trust him with your daughter." When Hai Chan, Kraft and Jo all stared at him, he continued, "I said I don't speak Spanish, but I do know enough to be sure *bebita* can't possibly refer to a boy."

"Pa?" Jo sounded a bit scared and Hai Chan couldn't blame her. She wouldn't be pretending to be a boy if she didn't have good reason.

Kraft took his daughter's hand. "Her ma died last year. Used up most of our spare cash, taking care of her. So I thought I could make our fortune, here in California. Or at least find work, where there weren't none back home. I couldn't leave Jo back there, though, so I thought if she pretended to be a boy, we'd be all right."

From Burns' way of talking earlier, Hai Chan had a feeling the disguise hadn't worked. "And the Reverend noticed?"

"I thought he was a man of God, he acts like a man of God. But he keeps trying to get her alone and keeps hinting that he knows." Kraft swallowed hard at the thought. "I don't like the way he talks, neither. Like he's offering to keep our secret if she goes with him. It ain't right. She shouldn't oughta be made to go with no man she don't want to."

Yi Xiao inclined his head. "I cannot possibly promise to protect her from every danger, but if you'll trust me as a traveling companion, I'll do my best to make sure she isn't harmed."

After a moment of hesitation, Kraft agreed. "Just don't get any ideas of your own, mister."

"That I can promise." Yi Xiao turned to look at the old woman, "You speak a little English. Enough to tell us where we can hire horses, and perhaps a mule or so?"

For a moment Hai Chan thought the woman would remain obstinately silent. Then she asked, "You have money?"

"I do. I think it's enough."

She considered him. Nodded approvingly. "You go out of town, up that hill just a little away and you find ranch. Tell them, Mama Imelda sent you. Tell them I say they sell you three horses, one mule." Before Yi Xiao could ask how she could be so sure they'd obey, she added, "Owner my grandson, Arturo Martinez. He do as he's told."

With a laugh, Yi Xiao bent over the lady's hand in a gesture he had to have learned from his father's second wife. "Mama Imelda, I do believe you're right."

ooo

Arturo Martinez proved to be as obedient to Madam Imelda's will as Yi Xiao was to his own grandmother's. Of course, Yi Xiao's payment, a hundred-tael silver boat, proved more than sufficient to convince him. Chinese money, in and of itself, wasn't useful in America, but silver was silver no matter where one went. Yi Xiao had had Burton go over American currencies, just to be sure, and knew enough to avoid being cheated too badly.

It was late afternoon by the time they finished negotiations. Arturo was an honest man and he insisted on giving them packs of food and equipment along with their mounts. It was just as well. Yi Xiao had his bedroll and Hai Chan had borrowed a blanket off the *Henrietta Marie*, but all Kraft and his daughter had was a bag of clothes. "I didn't want Burns to realize I was leaving," he explained, when Yi Xiao commented on his lack. "As it is, I'm afraid he'll notice what I did take and get suspicious."

It was an understandable concern. "Well, with luck, he'll be too busy trying to figure out how to convince Burton to let him aboard the *Henrietta Marie*."

"That's the boat you came on, right Yi Xiao?" Jo had climbed up behind her father and was peering back the way they'd come. San Diego's port was in sight from here and Yi Xiao had pointed out the *Henrietta Marie* where she'd docked. "Oh, she's moved."

The news surprised Yi Xiao only a little. Burton hadn't trusted Burns much more than he had. Scanning the port, he spotted the *Henrietta Marie* anchored in the middle of the bay, where it'd be even harder than before to approach her unnoticed. When he pointed her out, Hai Chan asked, "He's finished unloading already? That was fast."

"I think he wants to head for Panama as quickly as he can." Yi Xiao mounted his horse, a pleasant mare just a little bigger than the Mongolian pony he'd owned as a child. "The less time he stays, the less likely he'll have Burns trying to convince him to go to San Francisco."

Kraft coughed in an embarrassed way. "I think Reverend Burns might be just about done with convincing," he admitted. "He was making noises about using stronger means to persuade the next boat, earlier."

It sounded as if Yi Xiao and Burton had been right to worry about Burns. Hopefully Burton would make every effort to keep that man off his ship. According to Nana Grace, western clergy were supposed to be kind and gentle men. According to what Yi Xiao had seen in Burns' eyes, he was neither. Even worse if he really was trying to seduce young Jo.

Making their farewells of Arturo, and refusing to impose on him to start fresh and early the next day, Yi Xiao and his companions started up the El Camino Real. It was a dusty path that reminded Yi Xiao of some of the trails in the mountains of his homeland, albeit a bit wider and a great deal smoother.

The trees alongside the road were mostly odd looking oaks; all twisted and gnarled by the wind. There were scrubby little pines and a great deal of bushes whose species he didn't recognize. There was also a familiar feeling, a sense of being watched by something old and curious. Heng Shan had similar spirits, creatures bound to the elements, holding apart from the world of men.

Aside from that faint sense, the road was quiet, though Yi Xiao suspected it could be quite busy at the right time of day. He could see other

ranches, similar to the sprawling ranchero of their recent host. A few cat-
tle browsed along the roadway, disinterested in the presence of humans.
Somewhere high above, a huge bird circled and every so often Yi Xiao
thought he heard it call.

They traveled for several hours, to near dusk, before Kraft finally
begged a halt. "You two are used to riding, I can see that, but my legs feel
like they been pounded to ground meat. Besides, it's getting dark and Jo's
tummy's growling like a mad wildcat."

Alone, Yi Xiao could and would have walked a great deal further before stopping. They'd barely gone fifteen miles, after all. Still, he wasn't
alone or on foot. The horses couldn't travel in near darkness like he could
and his companions did seem to be getting tired. He found a place to
camp off to the side of the trail and pointed it out.

It only took a little while to set up camp. Even with Arturo's generous
help they didn't have much to work with. A blanket and a bedroll each, a
little pan for cooking and some provisions; dried meats and fruits, an odd
flour Arturo called maize, and a bag of beans. Arturo had made sure they
knew how to cook what they'd been given before they left, another kindness Yi Xiao appreciated. He'd have to remember to find a way to thank
both Arturo and Mama Imelda for their help.

Setting up a watch between the three adults—despite Jo's assurances
that she could help too—they settled in for the night.

ooo

Sleeping on land was never an easy thing for Hai Chan. He had no
trouble changing his walk to deal with solid ground but his body was accustomed to shifting waves. Bed for him was a constantly moving bunk
in a stuffy dark room that smelled of fish and human sweat. No matter
how tightly he shut his eyes or how much he shifted and moved to find a
comfortable position, he simply couldn't fall asleep. The constant breeze
flowing over him didn't help.

Thus he heard the faint sound in the darkness before Kraft did, even
with Jo's soft snoring. Something moved in the trees, a broken twig that
could have been cracked by an animal or a man. Either way, Hai Chan
didn't want to be snuck up on and he shifted again, moving as if he were
simply sleeping restlessly, and muttered nonsense under his breath.

Another sound, just as faint but a little closer, told Hai Chan he'd failed
to scare the stranger off. He shifted again, this time so he was facing away

from the fire. Eyes slitted just enough to see, he spotted a slim shadow amid the trees, moving slowly and cautiously towards them.

Something about the shape was familiar and Hai Chan flopped an arm out to poke Yi Xiao's foot. Or, rather, intending to poke Yi Xiao's foot. All he felt beneath his hand was the priest's bedding, rumpled and empty. Had he noticed Gan Han's approach and gone to surprise her? Or was he wandering around the woods in the dark? Knowing him, it was probably the latter.

Hai Chan's movement caused Gan Han to slow her steps. So she was sneaking up on them, perhaps intending to surprise Yi Xiao by being there when morning came, perhaps for less innocent purposes. Hai Chan didn't care which, because he had no intention of letting her do either. "Kraft, there's someone in the trees over there."

"Eh? What?" Kraft started upright and Hai Chan realized the man had been half-asleep. "Who? Where?"

Hai Chan sat up and glared in Gan Han's direction. She was just starting to back away when Yi Xiao came up behind her. "Oh, hello, Gan Han. Whatever are you doing here? I thought you were headed back to China."

The young woman slammed her elbow into Yi Xiao's chest, or where Yi Xiao's chest had been a second before. As usual, the priest's talent for worming his way out of trouble—physical or otherwise—meant the blow slid past him. "Damn you, Yi Xiao. Don't sneak up on me like that!"

"You were sneaking up on us," Hai Chan pointed out dryly, which earned him a sharp look. He was about to ask why Gan Han was there, instead of back aboard the *Henrietta Marie*, but movement behind Yi Xiao drew his attention and made him stop and stare wildly.

It wasn't human, for all it had a human form. No human stood so tall. No human was so utterly black as to reflect no light. No human had arms so long and thin. Jo squeaked at the sight and when Gan Han turned to see what they were staring at, she shrieked as well. She leapt backwards, practically falling over her feet to get away.

The shadow figure cocked its head, bending towards Yi Xiao. Hai Chan was about to leap forward and grab the idiot priest before he was eaten, but Yi Xiao simply reached up and touched the shadowy face with his customary lack of fear. In English, he told them all, "It's all right, everyone. He... she... I'm not sure which, is just a shadow."

"That isn't just shadows!" Hai Chan protested, watching the thing as it floated awkwardly around the camp. It didn't come properly into the light, but it seemed fascinated by the fire. "That's a monster!"

" DON'T SNEAK UP ON ME LIKE THAT. "

"It might be," Yi Xiao admitted. "Back home it'd be a kind of forest spirit, but I can't understand it well enough to tell if that's true here in America. I get the impression the folk around here call it a dark watcher."

"Is... is it going to eat us?" Jo asked, pressing close to her father for protection.

"I don't think so. Shadows follow the light, at least the ones back home do. It doesn't want to hurt us. They're usually harmless."

Usually harmless meant there was a chance of the opposite. Hai Chan didn't say so, not wanting to frighten the child. "Can you get it to go away?"

It already was. Having satisfied its curiosity about them, the shadowy figure stretched out an arm like a tree branch and patted Yi Xiao's cheek. The touch left a slight silvery mark against his skin, like the skeleton of a leaf. Then it was gone, leaving them all staring at Yi Xiao wildly.

"Well now, it being late and we having a long trip ahead of us, may I suggest we go back to sleep? Gan Han, you've obviously been walking all night. I won't ask you to take watch this time." Somehow they all fell in with Yi Xiao's plans without argument, a fact Hai Chan found almost as marvelous as the dark watcher itself.

OOO

It didn't surprise Yi Xiao to learn Gan Han hadn't bothered taking much in the way of supplies. When he pointed out her mistake she simply said, haughtily, "As soon as I defeat your blade I'm going to the nearest port and heading home. You brought water and food. What more do I need?"

They both knew she was overconfident. Not only was he not going to fight her, but her English was almost non-existent. Even if she did, by some stroke of fortune, defeat him, she'd little hope of finding a trustworthy captain to take her back to China. At least she'd managed to find suitable clothing. Like Yi Xiao and Hai Chan she was dressed in trousers and a loose shirt, a broad-rimmed hat covering her long hair and protecting her skull from the hot sun.

Still, she shouldn't have followed them. "Why in Lao Tzu's name didn't you just stay on the *Henrietta Marie*? And how did you find me, anyway?"

The questions made Gan Han turn away, staring at the road ahead. Softly, against her will, she muttered, "I was sent to fight you, to prove myself against you. I can't go home until I do."

This was the sort of nonsense citizens of the martial world insisted on making part of their lives. Yi Xiao understood filial piety. After all, he wouldn't be walking a long and winding trail along the Californian coast if he didn't. Yet filial piety that required a child to chase after a grown man so she could face his sabre in a meaningless duel? Surely no God would approve of it.

"You couldn't beat Tsang."

"He cheated with his magic. You may be a sorcerer like Hai Chan says, but...."

"I'm not a sorcerer and neither was Tsang. I saw you fight. You're good, excellent in fact. But you. Are. Not. My. Match." Her lips went tight and he tried another tack. "You have to duel me. Does it have to be with weapons? How about a nice game of mahjong?"

"Why can't it be weapons? Did you swear an oath? From what Burton told me, you already broke it, fighting Tsang."

The accusation was fair. "I didn't swear it, no. But I no longer seek the *dao*, but the *Dao*." She glared at him for the pun but he ignored her irritation, adding, "I'm a priest now. I've left the martial world...."

"There are monks and priests in the martial world and you know that as well as I."

She was right, too, though such men and women were often more interested in battle than they were in their faith. "True though that is, my master is not, and thus, neither am I."

"If you didn't swear an oath...."

"My sword is no longer the most powerful. Even if you did defeat me, you'd still have to defeat whomever took my place."

"I'm your closest rival, you damned fool! Just fight me, let me prove my worth, and I'll leave." She tried wheedling, "You refused aboard ship because I was still sick from Tsang's poison. I'm well enough now."

Yi Xiao refused to consider the possibility. "You still haven't told me how you found me."

"Your sabre led me to you."

"What?" The very idea was nonsense. "My sabre isn't magic. It has no mind or spirit to guide it to its rightful owner."

Sniffing disdainfully, Gan Han tapped the cloth hiding their weapons. "All blades grow attached to the one who wields them. I followed that attachment. Just like I followed you from Heng Shan."

Her certainty stunned Yi Xiao. If she were a trained sorcerer, or gifted with the kind of mind magic his mother's people often possessed, he'd have believed her right away. But she'd shown no signs of such skills before. Was she mad? Confused? Or did she really have such a talent?

"Well you can just stop following me. Take the sabre back to my grandmother. She'll know what to do with it."

"I. Will. Not."

It was likely the argument would have continued for some time if Kraft hadn't interrupted. "I'm not sure what all you folk are talking 'bout, nor why that girl's got such a mad on at you, but I've been trying to get your attention these last five minutes."

Yi Xiao apologized. "What's wrong?"

Both Kraft and his daughter pointed towards a cloud of dust off to the east. "There's someone, a whole lot of someones, coming down that road over yonder. I thought you'd like to know, cause they're moving pretty fast and they'll be here soon."

Even in the relatively peaceful countryside of his father's duchy, it wasn't a good idea to ignore strangers on the road. Yi Xiao grasped the reins of Gan Han's horse, and those of the mule. "Get to the side," he ordered. "Let's see who's coming. Gan Han, keep those weapons sheathed. I'd rather not get into a fight here."

ooo

The newcomers were all westerners, six white men and one black, all led by a lean older man who looked like he had all the patience in the world. They were dressed in leather boots, scuffed jeans, loose cotton shirts, and broad-rimmed hats. Pistols gleamed from their holsters, though Hai Chan wasn't sure what sort.

As soon as the new group reached the road the leader held up a hand to slow them down. If there'd been any sign of trouble, or aggression, there'd be a fight. Fortunately, despite Gan Han's yearning to prove herself, they all kept their hands to their sides.

The only one who remotely succeeded in appearing innocent was Yi Xiao. He gazed up at the newcomers with the wide eyed wonder of a child. The men's leader dismissed him immediately, obviously deciding Kraft was in charge. "You there. What's your name?"

It took Kraft a nervous second to respond, which worried Hai Chan. These men had the look of the local authorities. In his experience such men didn't like an apparent reluctance to cooperate. "Hal Kraft." With uncharacteristic spirit, Kraft added, "And yourself?"

The man eyed Kraft. "Jim Trendle," he finally said, sounding grim.

"And before you ask, I'm the law around here, so don't think about lying to me."

Kraft spread his hands, which caused his horse to shift uneasily. If Yi Xiao hadn't caught the reins from where he stood and whispered in the animal's ear, there would have been trouble. "S.. sorry. No. I'm no liar, Mister Trendle."

Hai Chan reflected the man had been lying about Jo earlier, but that was a different matter altogether. Seeing Gan Han about to say something, he reached over and caught her hand. "This isn't our business yet," he said urgently. "Don't interfere."

"That man is rude." She stared grimly at Trendle with a hard expression none of the men in his group liked.

"What's that little China girl mad about?"

Again Kraft stammered. "I'm not sure. I don't speak her language. She probably wants to keep moving. We do have a long trip ahead of us."

It would have been useful if Gan Han could put on the same sort of sweet, empty-headed, expression Yi Xiao was expert at. Useful for Hai Chan to do so as well, for that matter. Having no such ability, he contented himself with saying, in deliberately broken English, "We have long long way to go. Is trouble? We continue now, maybe?"

Trendle eyed Hai Chan, dismissing him without a word. "You're obviously not the ones we're looking for, but that doesn't mean you can't be helpful. Where did you come from and where are you headed?"

"San Diego to San Francisco." Before Trendle could ask why they hadn't taken a boat, Kraft added, "We tried to hire a ride, but the captains don't want to lose their crews to the gold fields."

One of the men behind Trendle laughed, "I heard the dock up San Francisco way is full up. They're having to ship supplies in by land from Los Angeles."

"What I want to know is why that little China girl is carrying a couple of great big pig stickers. She a butcher?" That was the large black man towards the back of the group. He was observant, Hai Chan would give him that much. The pig-stickers in question were covered in dark green silk and slung over Gan Han's back. Their shape was obvious, but only to one who knew weapons.

Trendle turned to Hai Chan. "Well, Chinaman?"

Cursing his luck, because he didn't want to be the center of attention, Hai Chan said, "She go meet husband to be. They gift. Male, female, blade. For wedding ceremony." There wasn't any traditional ceremony in China that used such props but he was sure Trendle and his companions couldn't know that.

After a moment, Trendle relaxed, returning his attention to Kraft. Hai Chan could see his disdain for the man's apparent cowardice. "Right. You're obviously not the ones we're looking for. But you be on the lookout, understood? There's a gang out here, been robbing the locals. You see anything, hear anything, you send word to me, got it?"

"Ah, yes, of course sir." Kraft hesitated. "Though it'd help if I knew what they were looking like?"

"Well, that's true," Trendle admitted. "There's about ten white men, led by a tall rangy fellow with a nose like a hatchet and a bad temper. One looks a bit like you, so be careful no one mistakes you for him."

"Yeah, like that'd happen," muttered one of Trendle's men. "This guy's got about as much much spine as a worm. No way he's Ginger Pete."

After a sharp look at his man for interrupting, Trendle added, "They're a nasty bunch. Murdered a whole family, all the way to the baby, over near El Cajon. Word is they've been heading north. So be careful and don't do anything stupid."

Kraft hurriedly and repeatedly assured Trendle that they wouldn't, leaving Hai Chan to wonder if anyone could make such a promise for a man like Yi Xiao.

ooo

Travel became easier further north. There were small ranches along the way, places to stop and buy food, and water the horses. They made good time, traveling around twenty-five to thirty miles a day. Yi Xiao had to walk alongside to allow Gan Han to ride, but he didn't mind. He enjoyed the extra effort. The air was fresh and clean, and if it smelled of strange plants and dust, it was warm and pleasant as well.

Gan Han continued trying to persuade him to duel her, but Yi Xiao ignored her efforts, knowing the rules required him to respond in kind. As long as he refused to face her she'd could do nothing but talk.

Walking through the scrubby little coastal forest, Yi Xiao let most of his mind drift, listening to the life in the woods as he'd been taught. He still wasn't good at it, not at all like his master. She could not only hear the spirits of the land, she could understand them. The closest he'd come had been the shadowy being he'd met earlier, and that only because it understood him better than he understood it.

Whatever it was, spirit, Immortal, forgotten God or even monster, it knew humans well enough to communicate its emotions. It'd liked him for some reason. Enough that it was somewhere out in the woods following him, its curiosity palpable despite the distance.

Several days after they'd met Trendle, Yi Xiao and his companions came upon a little ranch hidden among the scrubby trees. Like Arturo Martinez' place, it was a pleasant sprawling complex of buildings, all covered in that clay called adobe. Unlike Arturo's home, the building and yard were quiet and empty.

Yi Xiao could tell how wrong the silence was. A place like this ought to be bustling with activity, especially at mid-day. When he slowed to a halt, Hai Chan said, "Don't just stand there. We need water."

They needed to be safe and Yi Xiao was sure they weren't. He stopped the others, saying, "Let me go see if the owners mind our coming inside."

At least that was what he'd planned to say. Before he'd half-finished his sentence, a tall man came hurrying out the door, calling out cheerfully, "Welcome! Come on in!"

Hesitant, because he still didn't like the situation, Yi Xiao told him, "I think perhaps you've mistaken us for someone else. We're just travelers hoping to get some water before continuing on our way."

The man grinned, tobacco stained teeth jagged beneath a steel-grey mustache. "Now don't you worry none. We're not expecting nobody. It's just good hospitality and the fact we ain't seen another soul for a week. People don't usually stop in here, with that big old mission just up the road."

Most of the mission houses they'd passed on the way from San Diego had been shut tight or in use for other things. "I hadn't realized there were any still in operation. I'd been told they were closed down some years ago."

"That one's been turned to an inn. It's a nice place if you're looking to stop for the night. But why go walking another five miles when you can get water and food right here."

Kraft said, "It wouldn't hurt nothing to stop a little early, now would it?"

Seeing his companions didn't share his instinctive sense for trouble and willing to admit he might be wrong, Yi Xiao agreed, letting the man lead them inside, once their horses were settled with some hay and water out in the yard.

The central room of the ranch was big, a tall open space with comfortable looking furnishings and decorations of a sort Yi Xiao had never seen. Attractive hangings, a carved wooden jar, a shield with a heavy saber thrust behind it. It hung oddly, as if it were missing a blade. Their host coughed, gesturing towards an opening in the far wall. "If you'd like to come eat?"

Yi Xiao bowed politely but refused to be distracted. "Are you by yourself right now?" he asked, looking around for a servant or at least the man's family. There were signs everywhere that he had children, a few wooden toys dropped on the ground, a child-sized poncho woven of bright wool. "Did your children go visiting?"

The man blinked and Yi Xiao thought a flash of annoyance crossed his face. "My grandkids, you mean? Yeah, they went back to their ma just this morning. Still haven't had a chance to pick up after 'em. Rowdy lot they are, always making trouble." He grinned at Kraft, adding, "With hair like that, bet your boy's just as bad, right?"

Kraft chuckled, unware of, or ignoring, Yi Xiao's suspicions. "I'm afraid so, Mr...." he left the sentence hanging, letting their host finish.

"I'm Montgomery Jones. Just got this place recent. Haven't had a chance to get it started up proper." Jones explained. "Furnishing came with it, so don't bother asking me about it. Now come and make yourselves comfortable."

Guessing he'd get no more from Jones right then, Yi Xiao followed the man to the dining area. "A meal would be most welcome."

"We've got that covered, I promise." Jones paused to lean through a doorway, "Pete, get that food on the table quick. These people been on the road for quite a while."

They all sat down, Jones at the head of the table, smiling genially. Yet despite his friendly behavior and kindly manner, something about him still seemed strange. It took Yi Xiao several minutes before he realized the westerner wasn't reacting to him, or his fellow countrymen, the way most Americans had so far.

Admittedly, Burton had been equally polite but he'd been a stranger in a strange land at the time. Whereas it was Yi Xiao, Hai Chan and Gan Han who were the outsiders now. At the very least Jones ought to have remarked on the oddity of three Chinese on a trek through southern California. So far he hadn't turned a hair.

A man wearing a bandana came in carrying a bowl of some sort of soup. It smelled hot and spicy, though in an unfamiliar way that almost distracted Yi Xiao from his concerns. His sense of danger was growing, however, and he examined the man carefully as he served the food.

The cook, if cook he was, was thin and fine-boned. His skin was light, with a generous dusting of freckles to rival Jo's. His eyes were light brown, with a scar across one lid from a wound that must have come a hairsbreadth from blinding him. His hair was hidden beneath the bandana but it almost had to be bright red, given the color of his brows.

As Yi Xiao tasted the stew, or soup, or whatever it was, he recalled the name one of Trendle's men had mentioned a few days earlier. Pete. Ginger Pete. What was it about the name that reminded him of his second mother? Barely noticing the raw heat of the spices, or the way the others gasped, he searched his memory. "Oh!" he said. "Ginger means red haired!" Immediately, he could have cursed his fool mouth.

The announcement puzzled his companions but Jones and the man who had to be Ginger Pete glanced sharply at each other. A moment later they had guns out and had grabbed hold of both Jo and Gan Han. "Don't move or they get it!"

Yi Xiao wasn't surprised when Gan Han slammed her head back into Jones' face. An elbow to the chest was quickly followed by a stamp of a heavily booted foot that scraped straight down the man's shin. Jones screeched, trying to get his gun into position to fire. Before he could, Gan Han slid her sword from its sheathe. She was about to cut the man's throat for him when a glance at Yi Xiao made her stop.

"Damn you for being so soft," she muttered, slamming the hilt into Jones' temple. The man slid to the floor, unconscious.

Everything had happened so fast Ginger Pete didn't have a chance to react. By the time he opened his mouth to demand Gan Han stop it was too late. He stared at his compatriot, then turned a hot glare on Gan Han. "Nice moves, missy. But you can't stop me from shooting this boy. So just put that pigsticker of yours down and be quiet."

"Do as he says, Gan Han," Yi Xiao said in English, knowing she'd understand even if she didn't know all the words. When the girl glared at him, he gave her a pleading look. To his relief, she sighed and set the blade down on the table. She did not, he noticed, do the same with his sabre. It remained in its sheathe on her back, hidden by green silk.

"Now then," Pete said calmly. "I want you lot to go through that door, one at a time. You with the pretty talk, go first."

The man forced them through a hallway and Yi Xiao smelled something other than the spicy dish they'd been offered earlier. Blood and the stink of fear. He and Hai Chan glanced at each other, steeling themselves for what they were about to find.

They came to a door at the far end of the hall, where the smell was worse. There was a noise, too, a frightened little sound that might have crying. When Yi Xiao opened the door and stepped in, someone shrieked.

The room was a pantry, though most of the food had been thrown to the floor. It was full of children and young women; the real house-servants, working for whomever really lived here. Yi Xiao didn't like to think why they'd been spared.

"Get in there, all of you." Pete ordered and they obeyed unwillingly, crowding into the room. As the bandit dragged Jo back with him, her father tried to snatch at her arm. "Oh, no you don't," Pete snapped. "I'm keeping the boy with me. Just so you lot don't try anything stupid."

The door slammed shut, leaving them in darkness.

Hai Chan gave the bandit several minutes before he smashed the door open, letting a little light into the room. When Kraft protested, he pointed out, "That man's trying to get away. We probably trapped them inside, showing up when we did, and they meant to fool us long enough to escape. Besides, it's too damn close in here. I like cuddling, but not when the poor things are terrified out of their minds."

By this time Yi Xiao had slipped through the doorway. "What are you going to do?" Gan Han demanded. "I'm sure that man will injure the child if you show your face."

"I am going to sit down here in the hall," Yi Xiao announced calmly. "And we are all going to be quiet for a little while."

"More of your sorcery?" Hai Chan demanded.

"It's not sorcery." Yi Xiao slid into the cross-legged position he used when he was meditating. At the same time Kraft leapt past the man, tearing down the hall in a headlong rush. Sounding resigned, Yi Xiao added, "Keep an eye on him. Don't let him get his daughter killed."

Hai Chan set off running, with Gan Han close behind. "What is he up to?" the girl demanded as Hai Chan tried to figure out which way Kraft had gone. The house was a maze of hallways and he was thoroughly lost. An odd noise drew his attention and he cautiously opened the door to the room it came from.

"Gods."

What lay beyond had been a bedroom, once. Now it was an abattoir, filled with the fly covered remains of a half-dozen bodies. The ranch's menfolk, some hardly more than children, their throats slit and their fly-covered eyes wide and empty. An old man leaned against the wall, a sa-bre—twin to the one in the living room—thrust through his belly. He raised his head, staring blankly, and said something in Spanish that Hai Chan didn't understand.

"We can't help you," Hai Chan said gently, hoping the man understood English. "And there's someone else who needs us."

"Go," the man whispered. "Kill them."

"With pleasure," Gan Han growled from beside Hai Chan. "Let's go. I want my sword."

A sword was a poor weapon against a gun, but Hai Chan knew better than to argue. They continued searching and when they found the dining room, they both cursed. The sword was gone. Had the bandits taken it?

Gan Han closed her eyes. "It isn't far." Surprised, she added, "I think Kraft has it."

The girl had claimed she could follow a weapon's owner. Apparently the reverse was true as well. "Never mind, then. Unless your sorcery extends to stopping bullets, a sword isn't much use right now." Hai Chan could see how the accusation of magic infuriated her, but ignored her in favor of heading into the central room.

The sound of an argument drifted through the open windows and Hai Chan dropped to his knees, gesturing for Gan Han to do the same. To her credit and despite her annoyance, she obeyed. They crawled closer, listening intently.

"Telling you, we gotta get moving. That damned Trendle's onto us."

The voice was Montgomery Jones' and Gan Han growled a curse. "I should have killed him," she muttered.

"He can't know where we are," Ginger Pete said and more voices agreed with him. "Besides, I got this cute little hostage.... OW!"

At a guess, Jo had bit Pete as hard as she could. There were a few wild moments of shouts and bangs, ending with, "And stay there, you little brat!" The child had tried, but she hadn't managed to escape.

Hai Chan tried to decide what to do. Jo needed help but if he stuck so much as a hair into view those men would surely do him or her some damage. Gan Han looked equally helpless, her fists clenched tight at her sides.

A moment later something crashed through a door on the other side of the courtyard. "You let my kid go!" Kraft screamed furiously. As predicted, he was armed with Gan Han's sword; though it was obvious he'd no idea what he was doing. It was stupid, pointless and useless, but it was about the bravest thing the man had ever done. It gave Hai Chan the distraction he needed and he leapt through the wide open window, getting his bearings rapidly.

There were several men there, all turned to look at Kraft as he used Gan Han's sword to cut at the man holding his daughter captive. Pete had been startled just long enough to give Kraft a chance to stab him in the back of his hand, forcing him to drop his gun.

Catching hold of Pete by the back of the neck, Hai Chan flung him to the ground and grabbed Jo, tossing her back towards Gan Han. "Get inside," he ordered. "Gan Han, help me keep them out."

At the same time a shot rang out, setting Jo screaming. Hai Chan turned to see Kraft drop Gan Han's sword, hand going to his belly as he stared wildly at Montgomery Jones. He'd been so busy attacking his daughter's captor he hadn't noticed the man who'd shot him.

Hai Chan was strong. Strong enough to take injuries that would incapacitate most men. He was not stronger than a bullet. Instead of attempting to help a man beyond help, he dodged back inside, helping Gan Han drag Jo along.

"He killed my father! Let me at him. Give me a gun! I'll kill him!"

Hai Chan shook her. "This isn't the time for vengeance. We have to get out of here!"

With Gan Han's help, he dragged the screaming and crying girl back the way they'd come.

OOO

Yi Xiao didn't consider what he'd learned from the Hermit sorcery but he wondered if it was close. Gathering his *qi* and using it to command wind and water was one thing. Even using it to sense everything around him was part of that same skill.

This, however, was an extension of his abilities that pushed the definition almost out of shape. Connected to world around him, he could feel the movement of life as it ebbed and flowed. There, the terrified lives of the survivors. Here, the rapidly ebbing life-force of an old soldier who'd lost his final battle. There, his companions, searching for their quarry. Here, that quarry, too focused on his daughter's safety to protect himself.

And there, just outside, were twisted lives, glorying in bloodshed and the pain and fear they caused. Yi Xiao knew some of what they'd done had been for money, but a great deal of it had been love of cruelty. Their current victim, Jo, struggled against her terror, trying to find a chance to escape.

That moment came alongside something so terrible it almost shattered Jo's heart. Yi Xiao didn't need sight or sound to understand. He felt Kraft's movements, the way he'd closed with the twisted ones. Felt the moment of his death.

Jo's rescue was equally obvious and Yi Xiao thought they were safe enough now. They just had to escape the house and hide, at least until the men gave up. Given, of course, they would. Yi Xiao was about to put freshly cultivated *qi* energy to use protecting his companions when he felt the twisted ones turn gleeful.

A moment later there was an explosion and Yi Xiao realized the enemy's solution to their problem. They were going to burn everyone inside the building alive. There'd be no witnesses, no victims seeking vengeance. Just a pile of ash, smoking in the rubble.

If this were Heng Shan, whose elements Yi Xiao had long practiced connecting to, he could have drawn down a storm to douse the fire. Here, however, he'd barely begun to scratch the surface of this land's elements. He'd no hope of commanding air so dry and still.

Something moved at the edge of Yi Xiao's thoughts. The dark watcher, observing what he did and curious as always. Could it help? Would it help? Calling it took all Yi Xiao's attention, so he was only dimly aware of his companions returning and babbling about the fire.

"Master says, when in danger, panic leads to self-destruction," he said without opening his eyes. "Be quiet. I'm asking for help." Neither Hai Chan nor Gan Han understood but they didn't argue, letting him focus all his attention on the dark watcher.

They connected; a deeper and more intimate connection than before. The dark watcher, or watchers, were ancient. So old the ones who'd called them into being were long gone. Now the forest, the great huge trees that had been their homes, were gone, leaving them to wander alone and lonely, through a changed landscape.

Yi Xiao dared not offer hope. He didn't even know what would help these ancient beings. He did offer friendship, even a kind of companionship, should they desire it. At the same time he pleaded, showing the beings what was happening, showing them the killers and their victims. Showing them the fiery death awaiting him and his companions if nothing were done.

Wood moved. The trees around the ranch shifted, twisting their way free of the dry and rocky dirt. Drawn along with the spirits, Yi Xiao sensed the killers and hungered for their end.

Someone screamed, then another, as his new allies tangled their roots and branches around the murderers.

Yi Xiao focused his attention on one in particular. Montgomery Jones. If he had let Gan Han kill him, Kraft might still be alive. Without hesitation, without so much as a qualm, he set his allies on the man, twisting their branches around his neck in a grotesque and appropriate hangman's noose. Jones screamed and went silent a moment later.

"Now, make an exit," Yi Xiao whispered. "Quickly."

The nearest wall buckled and crumbled away as hundreds of tendrils tore the clay apart. Then they pulled back from the flames, and Yi Xiao opened his eyes. "Out of the house. Now."

ooo

Escaping the burning ranch required Hai Chan and Gan Han to chivy the terrified servants from the 'safety' of the pantry and through a shattered wall. To Hai Chan's surprise, what calmed the frightened women wasn't the fresh air and sunlight. Rather it was the sight of the bandits who'd attacked them, trapped within within the branches of the same trees that had torn up the courtyard and the building's wall.

They seemed particularly pleased by the corpse dangling above them. Nor did Hai Chan blame them. He'd seen Jones' victims. Hanging had been the least of what he'd deserved.

"It's going to be quite a time getting them out," Hai Chan commented.

"I'm just glad only Jones died." Yi Xiao's sentiment wasn't shared by anyone else, but Hai Chan knew how hard the young priest yearned to break with his upbringing. Right then he was holding Jo in his lap, letting the girl cry, his eyes distant as he watched Gan Han gather their things so they could go on. "Spirits like the dark watchers don't have the same morality we humans do. But it was I who asked it of them."

Hai Chan wasn't one to judge. His own morality was barely better than the dark watchers'. It certainly wasn't as noble as Yi Xiao was trying to become. The survivors weren't the only ones viciously pleased by Jones' fate. "What do we do now?" He didn't think they could just walk away.

"We'll send someone to find Trendle. Once he's here, he and his men can have their quarry." Yi Xiao patted Jo on the head, adding, "Not to mention finding a family to take our young lady here in. Once that's done, we can continue to San Francisco. I'm in no rush, but I'm sure you want to get back to sea again."

"...TANGLED THEIR ROOTS AROUND THE MURDERERS."

It was a truth Hai Chan didn't need to confirm. He enjoyed Yi Xiao's company. Was even beginning to appreciate the man's sorcery, or whatever he insisted on calling it. But he was a sailor, first and foremost.

And a sailor belonged on the sea.

Chapter 4: Fire –
The Goal in Sight brings Progress

They buried Jo's father in the same churchyard as the rest of Pete Grubb's victims, on a hillside overlooking the Pacific. She thought he'd like that. He'd liked watching the sun setting over the ocean. Said it put him in mind of the way her Ma would shell peas, sitting on the stoop in the evening.

Once her Pa was properly settled, Jo made it clear she wanted to stay with Yi Xiao and his companions. "Everyone around here talks Spanish," she pointed out when Yi Xiao tried to persuade her otherwise. "And that Trendle fellow don't need a kid hanging round him."

Yi Xiao might act like a damnfool, but he had a sharp way about him that saw through Jo's excuses. There were a few English speaking families in the little town nearby. She could have stayed with them if she'd wanted and they both knew it.

To her relief, all he said was, "I'm not a good choice for a father, but I am expert at being a big brother." That made Gan Han snort, proving the girl understood English better than she pretended. "Still, you should know I have a way of running into trouble whether or not I try to avoid it. Will you allow me to teach you to defend yourself?"

Jo understood. She'd gotten herself used as a hostage back at that ranch. If she could have fought back, or at least done a better job of escaping, her Pa might still be alive. "Will you teach me how to use a sword? I already know how to handle a gun."

"I will not." His refusal irritated Gan Han but she didn't say a word, just drew her sword, raising it towards Yi Xiao's throat. He pushed it aside without effort, adding, "Nor will I fight you."

For Jo's sake Gan Han answered in heavily accented English. "You will. Sooner. Later. You will."

Somehow, Jo had a feeling Yi Xiao had more stubborn in his little finger than Gan Han had in her whole body. She didn't understand the pair's relationship at all; it seemed obvious to her Gan Han must be in love with Yi Xiao. But they played the same sort of game some of the older kids did back home, pretending to hate each other. Or, at least, Gan Han did. It was hard to imagine Yi Xiao hating anyone.

After the burial they were on their way again, wending their way through dry, brush covered hills and scrubby pine forests. Every morning Yi Xiao practiced that odd dance he called a fighting style, trained Jo to defend herself, then continued towards San Francisco.

It didn't take long before Jo noticed Yi Xiao going distant every so often. Sometimes he said he was communing with the land. Sometimes he said he was cultivating—whatever that meant—his *qi*. But other times he just looked sad, like there was something eating at him.

Jo did ask why he looked that way, but the only answer he had was, "Master says, the heart's fire can be harnessed, but never doused."

It meant nothing to Jo, but Gan Han muttered something in Chinese Jo was pretty near sure wasn't complementary. Jo was trying to learn the language, but there were things her companions wouldn't teach her. The best she could guess was that Yi Xiao's mood had something to do with the reason why Gan Han kept trying to fight him. She didn't understand what they meant by a martial world but she didn't have to know to realize it ate at Yi Xiao something fierce.

Whenever Jo saw that look on Yi Xiao's face, she tried to distract him with questions about his home and family. He didn't talk much about his parents but he had a great deal of fun telling her all about the troubles he'd get into with his brothers and sisters.

"How'd you avoid getting beaten?" Jo asked, after one elaborate tale about how he, his half-sister and his older brother had climbed the supporting pillars of some temple and gotten stuck.

"Oh, we didn't avoid it. We weren't sitting for a week after they got us down. But that was nothing, compared to the time my cousin and I switched places. I was nearly killed."

That made Jo's eyes go wide. "How'd you manage that?"

Ruefully, Yi Xiao scrubbed his hand through his thick hair, the short locks sticking up all over, "Someone thought I was him." Embarrassed, he muttered to himself, "Master says, a patched wine-jar doesn't leak. I shouldn't have brought up the subject."

"Now that you have, you may as well finish," Hai Chan pointed out. "You have me curious. Gan Han, too."

"Not include me in nonsense." Gan Han pretended to look away, as if she didn't care. But Jo could tell she was interested, despite herself. Interested enough to speak in English so Jo could understand.

"Well, yes. I suppose." Yi Xiao considered his words carefully. "My cousin and I look a great deal alike. Some people even think we're twins. We're not, of course, for all we were born on the same day and in the same place."

A cold snort escaped Gan Han's lips. "Given who cousin is, see why that problem." She paused, adding, "That why they exile you?"

"I'm not exiled," Yi Xiao denied. "But it is why I've been sent away." He looked west, like he thought he could see all the way to China. "Maybe someday, when things settle down, I can go home. Right now all I can do is hope my cousin's all right. Him and all my family."

ooo

It was mid-morning, over three weeks after they'd left San Diego, when Yi Xiao spotted the tip of what had to be San Francisco Bay. By this time they'd begun seeing more and more people using the same road they were on. Californios, Mexicans, the occasional native, white men and black and a few other Chinese.

"Why won't they smile at you," Jo asked suddenly as the third group of Chinese prospectors passed. As bright and sharp-eyed as she was, she couldn't fail to notice the way they avoided Yi Xiao's gaze.

"They probably don't like my face." At Gan Han's dour chuckle, Yi Xiao added in Chinese, "Oh, you do have a sense of humor after all?"

"It's not your face they don't like, you know."

"I know. But do you really want me to give the young lady a history lesson?" The trouble wasn't Yi Xiao's face, but his ancestry. Most of the Chinese immigrants to America were Han, with some enclaves of other Chinese minorities. Yi Xiao might lack his people's traditional shaved forehead, but his Manchurian ancestry was obvious.

"She's bright. You don't need to hide truths from her."

Gan Han might be obsessed and stubborn as their pack mule on one subject but she was right about Jo's intelligence. The girl had sharp eyes and learned quickly. In English again, he told her, "China has a long history of dynasties rising and falling. It also has dozens of different peoples. Miao, Han, Mongolian, Manchu.... the list is huge, especially if you go further west. Right now the ruling family—the Qing—are from the Manchu people. But prior to that, the Ming ruled, and they—like most of the immigrants here—were Han."

Jo caught on quickly. "So they don't like you because you're Manchurian?"

To be honest, Yi Xiao thought some of them had better reason than that. "Ruling classes are seldom well-loved by those they rule," he noted. "I'm not really all that important... be quiet, Gan Han... just a priest searching for understanding. But they can't know that." It'd be different if he were Buddhist. Their shaved skulls were easily recognized and mostly respected.

They continued riding along a hillside that grew taller and taller as they went. More hills rose around them, hiding the bay. Buildings started to appear, square temporary structures more like tents than anything else. If they were tents, they seemed odd to Yi Xiao's eyes. He'd visited his grandfather's clan in Manchuria once, when he was young, and had fond memories of the lovely round yurts dotting the grassland.

As they rounded a bend, Yi Xiao scanned the scene ahead of them. The hillside was covered in more buildings overlooking a bay so full of boats it was almost impossible to see the water beneath. It was an amazing sight, leaving him wondering if one could just walk across by leaping from boat to boat.

Even as Yi Xiao contemplated the possibilities, Hai Chan grinned and clapped his hands together. "You see?" he told them. "All I have to do is find a crew."

OOO

San Francisco was a cacophony; shouts, things banging into other things, metal ringing on metal. It was a bewildering mix of odors; meat, burning wood, tar, coal and other things far less savory. It was a blur of colors and people; all moving to and fro about their business. Jo wanted to run wild, to explore every nook and cranny of the place. If her father had been alive she'd have tried, knowing he'd trust her not to wander far. Yi Xiao might not, seeing himself as her guardian as he did.

The road ahead grew steep, leading to a series of larger and better constructed buildings. They were nothing compared to the brick and glass houses back home in Shanksville, but they were a sight better than the rough tent structures covering the hillside.

Just like on the road, there were all sorts of people in San Francisco. Most looked like prospectors taking a break from their work. Others seemed to be shopkeepers or the like, all going about their business with barely a curious glance at the strangers wandering their town. Newcomers like Jo and her companions were likely common as weeds and just as interesting.

There was one fellow caught Jo's eye, but before she could point him out to Yi Xiao the man disappeared around a corner. It had nothing to do with them, but it was funny to see someone wearing that haircut Yi Xiao'd mentioned, the one Manchurians preferred back in China. He was oddly dressed, too, in a long dark robe with shiny embroidery, big sleeves and a high collar. There being other Chinese wandering around San Francisco, Jo guessed it didn't matter. He was probably just stopping in town for supplies or a rest.

By then they were close to what looked like a main street. There was a greengrocer of sorts, a dry-goods place, a land office, a bank and—about halfways down—an inn. She pointed it out. "Should we get rooms?"

"It's only mid-afternoon," Yi Xiao answered. "Are you really that tired?"

"There are people arriving all the time, least that's what my uncle Caleb said when he wrote Pa. If we're going to be staying, we gotta strike while the iron is hot."

Blinking, Yi Xiao considered her words. "I understood that one. All right, if you think it'd be better, I can't see a good reason to refuse." He said a few words to Gan Han, who shrugged without argument. They left the horses tied with a half-dozen others and set Hai Chan to keep an eye on their things.

Inside, the inn was dark but clean. The man behind the desk was neatly dressed and looked pleasant enough, but his expression changed as Yi Xiao walked closer. "No havee roomee for you. You go, find Chinee place. Stay there."

It hadn't occurred to Jo that there'd be a problem. Of course, back home she'd never seen a Chinese, anymore than most of her people had. No one would have known what to make of Yi Xiao, but they would have been polite. Well, most of them would be.

Yi Xiao stopped at the desk and smiled broadly at the innkeeper. "I'm sorry. I'm not familiar with that dialect." he said in that crisp sharp English of his. "Or is it a speech impediment?" At the same time he set one of those oddly shaped silver lumps his people called money on the desk between him and the man. It was one of the bigger ones, its surface glittering in the lamplight, the shape of a Chinese word stamped at its center.

The innkeeper stared at the money. "I do apologize sir. I mistook you for...." Flustered, he fell silent. They all knew he'd done nothing of the sort. "What sort of rooms are you looking for? And for how long?"

"Two, for a few days—until we get settled. Preferably next door to each other. You may put us towards the back of the inn, if need be, but not right over the kitchen please."

Having determined that real money was involved, the innkeeper bowed. "They aren't very large, but I have two such rooms on the third floor." He hesitated, "It's an attic, but I promise it's clean and kept proper."

"Excellent. Is a bath included?"

"Yes, sir," the man answered quickly. "Only space for one in each room, but I'll have them refilled as soon as need be, if you like?"

"I would be most appreciative." Yi Xiao bowed. "And, while I have your attention, would you happen to know where I can find a Mr. Chang in this city?"

The question set the innkeeper staring. "Near as I can tell, there are dozens. They all live over in the Chinese district, up the way some." He pointed off to the west, towards the hillside.

"Then that is where I shall start. Just as soon as we've settled in." Yi Xiao paused to ask Hai Chan to stable the horses, then led the way upstairs.

The rooms turned out to be small and dimly lit. Servants' quarters, no doubt, and hardly worth the amount of silver Yi Xiao had paid for them. If it'd been Jo's Pa, or Reverend Burns, there'd have been an argument on the subject. Yi Xiao just smiled ruefully, when she told him so, saying, "I expected his reaction."

"Why didn't you argue none with him, then? That was a lot of money you paid."

"Master says, money is a fine tool but a poor paving material."

Gan Han muttered something under her breath as she examined the bed for bugs. "Why ask Chang? Common name."

Yi Xiao moved out of the way of the servants bringing the baths and buckets of hot water to their rooms. "I know. But I wanted to know where the local Chinese are living. Without being told to go stay with them again."

It still bothered Jo, the way that man reacted to her guardian. "Why would he? Your money's good."

"And I'm a stranger in a strange land." By now Hai Chan was thumping up the stairs to join them. "You grew up in a remote town out in the country. No one taught you to think Chinese are barbarians. Our host, on the other hand, likely believes that very thing. That's why, despite paying enough to get us into the best room in the best hotel in San Francisco, we are here in these tiny rooms and grateful they're at least well-kept."

Hai Chan looked into the room he'd be sharing with Yi Xiao. "They're better than my bunk aboard the *Southern Cross*, at least." He tossed his bag in a corner and headed back outside. "I'll go check out the ships. Gods know what condition some of them are in." Before Jo could ask what he was going to use to pay for a whole ship, he was gone. With a shrug for their companion's abrupt disappearance, Yi Xiao went into his room and closed the door.

"Child, bathe first." Gan Han ordered.

"I'm all right," Jo told her roommate, though she knew she didn't smell too good. "I've got to go look for someone myself." Then, like Hai Chan before her, she hurried downstairs, hoping Gan Han wouldn't go all maternal on her, trying to keep her out of trouble.

ooo

A hot—or relatively hot—bath was a rare luxury and Yi Xiao took gleeful advantage of an even rarer moment of solitude to soak in its heat. This was the first time he'd been properly alone since he'd left Heng Shan and he reveled in the quiet. Well, mostly quiet. The noise of the streets outside was a faint rumble of bangs, clangs and curses. Distant and muffled as they were, he barely noticed.

It was almost half an hour later when Yi Xiao realized his charge was missing. He'd finished his bath, dressed and tapped on Gan Han and Jo's door, intending to tell them he was going out.

Gan Han answered, wrapped in a sheet from her bed and annoyed at the interruption. "I've no clue where she went. She said something about finding someone and ran off. She's a big girl. I'm sure she's fine."

Yi Xiao wasn't so sure. Gan Han had grown up in the martial world. She'd been defending herself from bullies and the like for most of her life. She could have walked through the worst districts of Shanghai or Hong Kong without much risk.

Jo, on the other hand, had only two weeks of limited self-defense training to protect her. She was smart, hopefully smart enough to run from what she couldn't fight, but she was also impetuous and hot-tempered. Yi Xiao could imagine her saying or doing the wrong thing in the wrong place all too readily. "I'll go look for her." He hurried outside, pausing only long enough to ask the innkeeper which way the child had gone.

Gan Han was dressed and following Yi Xiao before he got more than a dozen steps away from the inn. "Why are you so worried?"

"She's a child."

"She's a year younger than I am."

"You're a child too."

"I. Am. Not."

Yi Xiao ignored her in favor of asking a man fixing a wooden sign, "Did you see a red-haired boy come through?"

"That I did. Asked where the post office was." The fellow pointed down the street. "The building with the flag up top. Can't miss it."

Yi Xiao hoped that was true and tossed the man one of the coins he'd gotten from Arturo back in San Diego. He was about to continue when something caught hold of his shoulder and spun him around. "Where's the girl?" Reverend Burns hissed into his face furiously. "And don't play dumb, Chinaman. I already know you speak English."

ooo

The post office wasn't much of a place, but Jo figured it didn't need to be. It was also almost empty, with just three men working behind the desk packing up boxes of envelopes. The oldest of them looked up at her sharp, "Ain't been no mail yet, boy. That new ship just come in from China, of all places. They got nothing for the likes of you."

Jo smiled, imitating Yi Xiao at his most engaging. "Naw sir, I ain't here for mail." At the same time she wondered why a boat had come from China. For that matter, why hadn't Yi Xiao and the others taken a straight trip to San Francisco if one was available?

"Got a letter to send, then? Where's it going? Further away, more it costs."

Jo walked on up to the desk. "Not a letter, neither," she admitted. "I was told you got post boxes here?"

The man agreed on that. "You better have your pa take care of renting one, though. I can't be doing business like that with a kid."

"Ain't renting. Picking up. Here, I got a letter saying I can." Jo pulled out the envelope she'd been carrying all the way from Shanksville. Pa had thought it'd be safer with her. She could move fast and hide better than him, if anyone tried to take it. Besides, who'd think a kid like her would have anything valuable?

The clerk took the letter and read it careful. Then he took the little key at the bottom of the envelope. "Well, I guess it's in order," he allowed. "Give me a moment. That box is way in the back and it's a tight squeeze."

"I'll just wait over there," Jo told him, pointing to a corner where she could look out the window. "Out of the way."

The street outside was as fascinating as ever and Jo tried to imagine what sort of people were passing by. Some looked like they'd been soldiers, once upon a time. They walked straighter, with a confident air. Some had been around for a while, ambling along without a care in their world. And, of course, the newcomers were obvious. They stared wide-eyed at everything, taking it all in.

A familiar figure walked past the building. The same Chinese man she'd seen earlier. He strode along confidently, ignoring the way passersby stared at his odd clothes. Now she saw him up close, she could see he was clean-shaven, a little older than middle-aged, and sternly handsome. He had the look of a man used to being obeyed, like a soldier or something. Jo wondered who he was and why he'd seemed to recognize their group. Was he from that ship the clerk had mentioned?

To Jo's surprise, the man turned and walked straight into the post office, dark eyes scanning the room until they found her. "Well, hello there. Was that you I noticed with my countryman earlier?" His English wasn't as polished as Yi Xiao's, but it was excellent, nonetheless.

He seemed nice and polite and Jo relaxed. "Yes, sir, that was me."

"It's terribly rude of me, of course, but could you tell me your companions' names? I've a feeling I know them and would like to be sure. It's been some time since I saw them last, after all."

Jo didn't see any reason to stay silent. "The tall one is Hai Chan. The short one is Yi Xiao and the lady is Gan Han. I'm just finishing my business here, I could take a message to them, if you'd like." By this time the clerk had come out from the back room with her package.

The man smiled in a genial way. "You could take me back to meet them, instead. I'd like that even better." He waited for her to sign the clerk's log book and put her package in her bag. "If it wouldn't be too much of an imposition?"

There didn't seem to be a reason why she shouldn't. She'd taken longer than she'd meant to and she needed to hurry back anyway. "All right, mister. I suppose that's fine. It's not far, just about five minutes away. Maybe a bit more, with that hill out there."

They walked up the steep street, the man apparently oblivious to the noise and fuss surrounding them. He was more interested in Jo's relationship to Yi Xiao. "You're obviously not blood kin to him. How is it you're with him? Surely you have family?"

Jo didn't want to explain too much about herself and wasn't sure what her companion wanted to know. Her Pa once said if there was a hinge on her tongue she'd rattle on both ends. It got worse when she was anxious and this tall, powerfully built, man was just the sort to make her nervous. "I got separated. He's helping me out 'til I find my family."

They weren't far from the inn when Jo spotted the first sign of trouble. Reverend Burns' assistant, Joel—the one who never bathed and seldom brushed his teeth—was just heading into alleyway. And if he was there, surely that meant Burns was as well.

"Is something wrong?"

Jo spotted Yi Xiao and Gan Han talking to a man working on a sign. Yi Xiao tossed the man a coin and was about to move on when Burns appeared from between two buildings. As the man caught hold of Yi Xiao's shoulder, more of Burns' men came out quietly to surround the pair. It was done so smooth no one around Yi Xiao and Gan Han noticed. Or if they did, they made nothing of it and left the group alone.

Jo stepped behind her companion and watched as Burns spoke sharply to her friend. He towered over Yi Xiao, glaring down intimidatingly and Jo waited for Yi Xiao to use his skills to break free. To her surprise, he didn't. Instead he cocked his head in that annoyingly foolish way of his and went with Burns, letting the man drag him off to God knew where.

"Come on, mister," she gasped to her new companion. "I don't know what's going on but I know that fellow's trouble. Yi Xiao needs help."

OOO

"Why are you letting this man drag us off where he likes?"

"Tell that girl to stop talking Chinee and speak like a real person," Reverend Burns snapped, glaring down at Gan Han as he dragged them both by the elbow through the streets.

"Her English isn't very good," Yi Xiao explained, giving Gan Han a warning look. "She wants to know why I'm cooperating."

"You're cooperating 'cause I'm gonna beat your yellow hide black and blue if you don't, you little bastard."

"Oh, I sincerely doubt that." Yi Xiao gave Burns the sweetest smile he could muster. "I don't think you could afford it, anyway."

One of the other men, the one with the bad teeth and worse breath, asked, "Afford? What's there to afford?"

"I charge for damage," Yi Xiao explained. "If you hit me and the blow lands, you pay me." He considered the matter thoughtfully while their captors stared at him. "Though I must admit, I haven't worked out the going rates here in America."

Gan Han kicked at his ankle but he slid his foot out of the way before she connected. "Idiot! Turtle's Egg!" she growled. "Must you?"

"Well, yes, I must. After all, if they manage to hurt me I'm going to need medical aid." Yi Xiao spoke in English so he couldn't be accused of conspiring.

"If you don't shut your damned mouth you'll be needing an undertaker," Reverend Burns snapped. "Now be quiet until we're someplace private."

They continued to the edge of the bay, where dozens of warehouses stood alongside the docks. Rounding the north end, Yi Xiao could see an island with a few buildings, and a spit of land rising into a densely wooded hillside. One of the men shoved at him to get his attention and he shifted his shoulder just enough to send his attacker stumbling forward when he missed.

"Stand still!"

"Not until I've worked out how much to charge. For that matter, even if I did know how much I was going to charge I wouldn't stand still. There's no reason to make it easy for you." Yi Xiao let Burns lead them into an old and crumbling warehouse at the very edge of the pier. "How charming. Is this where you gentlemen are staying? And however did you get here ahead of us? I do hope you didn't manage to capture the *Henrietta Marie* after all."

"We didn't get here before you, you stupid bastard. We've been just behind you the whole way." Something about the way Burns spoke suggested the delay wasn't according to plan. The only reason they'd taken so long was because they'd only just caught up. "Now where's Kraft and his girl? Did you lose 'em somewhere? Maybe steal that letter of theirs?"

Yi Xiao was puzzled. "Letter?" he asked. "What letter?"

Jo's voice came from the darkness at the other side of the warehouse. "The one my uncle sent us before he died, giving Pa a share in his mine up in Heavenly Valley."

oOo

Two weeks training wasn't good enough to go up against Burns and his friends and Jo knew it. She was glad she had someone backing her up. Belatedly, she realized she didn't know anything about the fellow, much less if he'd help. But he'd followed along readily when she'd said Yi Xiao was in trouble, so he couldn't be anyone bad.

They all stared on each other, taking everyone's measure. Jo could tell Burns wasn't bothered by her sudden appearance, or her companion. He didn't think much of anyone who wasn't a white man, of course, so likely figured the Chinese man to be nothing more than a nosey local prying where he wasn't wanted.

"Mine, Jo? You never mentioned any mine?" Typical of Yi Xiao, he might have been asking the time.

Two could play Yi Xiao's game. Jo answered as lightly as he, "I'm sorry. I shoulda told you back when Pa got killed. My Ma's brother was working for Mr. Sutter when they found gold. He was one of the ones earned enough to do something with, so him and his partner got a bit of property somewhere north of here, out in the hills. He willed my Pa his share in the profits."

"Profits your father promised.... Wait... he's dead?" Burns stared.

"Mr. Kraft was killed by bandits somewhere near... Los Angeles, I think it was?" Yi Xiao explained.

"That means...."

"That means the share belongs to me, Reverend Burns." Jo looked firm on the man, not at all willing to give an inch. He was a bully, always insisting on his own way and Jo was tired of him.

"You're a child. A little girl," Burns sneered, adding, "Oh, I'm sorry. Did I reveal something you didn't want known?"

Since even the fellow behind Jo wasn't surprised, she just said, "It don't matter. I'm the only one left in my family. I'll fight you for it...."

Yi Xiao interrupted. "Child, I haven't taught you nearly enough to duel with."

"I mean in court. Reverend Burns and I got no blood tie. He's just one of the group we were traveling with. He got no say in what happens to my Pa's property." Jo wasn't experienced in the world but she knew her rights.

If Burns could have set Jo alight right then and there, he'd have done it. She knew he didn't like being thwarted and a girl thinking she could say 'no' to him was about the worst thing ever. She wondered how many people had to have let him have his way for him to get like this. Too many, that was sure.

Somehow, despite his fury, Burns kept his temper. "Your father owed me for helping you two get as far as you did. Or are you forgetting I'm the one had the quinine that saved your life?"

That was as maybe and Jo said as much. "Pa's gone, though."

"I'LL FIGHT YOU FOR IT..."

"Dead or no, he promised me a share of what was waiting for him here in California. So if you're the one owns that bit of property of your uncle's—and until there's a deed put in your name, you ain't—you owe me what he did."

"You forced him to make that deal while I was sick. When he didn't have no choice." Jo still felt guilty over that. It was her fault her Pa had agreed at all.

"But he did make it, girl. You know it, just as well as I. And I'm not being greedy and asking for the whole thing." Burns spread his hands, smiling beatifically. "I promise, I wasn't cheating him none and I'm not cheating you."

It didn't seem right and it didn't seem fair. It especially didn't seem right when Yi Xiao said softly, "Master says, a debt forgotten hangs on the soul." He slipped past Burns and his men before any of them could notice and walked up to Jo.

"I don't care if he says he's a man of God. I been watching him this whole way and he's a dirty, no good, scoundrel."

Yi Xiao set a light hand on her shoulder. "He may not be a good man. He may frighten you. But he hasn't wronged you. If your father owed him, you shouldn't refuse the debt for those reasons."

Jo wanted to argue but she couldn't find an adequate defense. Helplessly, she told Burns. "What did Pa promise, for that quinine?"

"There's a box up on that property of your uncle's, hid in a cave. It's got something special in it, meant for your father. You give us that, we're even."

"From the sound of things, we need to go to the property and find whatever it is Jo's uncle left." When Burns opened his mouth to object, Yi Xiao raised a finger to stop him. "Do you know what's in the box? No, I see you don't."

Burns didn't look at all pleased at the argument. "Don't test me!"

"I most assuredly am not," Yi Xiao answered. "But it'd be disappointing if all the box contained were a few family mementos, of no value to anyone but Jo." Seeing Burns wilt, he added, "If I may suggest, find a place to stay for the night. Tomorrow we will replenish our supplies and head to Mr. Kraft's...."

"Uncle Caleb was a Yancey, Yi Xiao."

"....Mr. Yancey's property and discover what was left for Jo's father."

There being nothing more Burns could say on the matter without starting a fight, the man accepted the suggestion.

○○○

Yi Xiao sent Jo and Gan Han back to the inn. "You might see where we can eat. I'll be along in a little while."

Neither girl liked the suggestion, especially since Yi Xiao deliberately phrased it like an order. But they didn't argue the point, either. Once they were gone, Yi Xiao turned his attention on the man who'd been silently hovering behind Jo like a large carrion bird. Given, of course, carrion birds dressed in the heavily embroidered silk robe of an Imperial court official.

"Your Highness," the man said, going to one knee, despite the dirt and rust on the warehouse floor. "I hoped I would reach here before you."

The honorific was one Yi Xiao had no right to. "I'm no prince. There's no need to stand—or kneel—on ceremony with me. I'm not even sure who you are?"

"Your Highness is pleased to jest with me."

It wasn't hard to work out what was going on. This man, whomever he was, was an official of the Imperial Court. No doubt he'd been sent to find and bring Prince Yi Zhu back home, only to be fooled by the same trick Grandmother Lang had used on General Hwei.

Yi Xiao could play along, let this strange man take him home as he obviously intended. But that would mean pretending to be his cousin. It'd be fatal, because—if the rumors of the Daoguang Emperor's dying were true—by now Yi Zhu had either taken his rightful place as Emperor or had fallen in the attempt. Impersonating him would be treason either way. Whomever sat upon the Dragon Throne could not afford to have Yi Zhu's 'twin' cousin roaming free.

"What is your name?"

"I am Wang Tsun Hsin, your Highness." Wang refused to raise his head or unclasp his hands. "Please, accept my humble service and allow me to assist you in returning home. Your father needs you desperately."

"When did you leave China?"

"But a few hours after you, your Highness. We followed your ship, but a storm forced us off course. I had our Captain head for San Francisco, in hopes that we'd find you here. Thank the Gods, we have!"

The man's sincerity was heart-warming. It was also damned inconvenient. "Whatever and whomever I may be in China," Yi Xiao said finally, "I am Lang Yi Xiao here."

If Wang hadn't been an official at court and therefore trained from an early age to submit to the will of the Emperor, he might have questioned Yi Xiao's statement. Instead he bowed deeply. "Your Highness has but to will it."

"And so I do. I am also not ready to return to China."

"But your Highness...."

"Don't call me that." Yi Xiao pulled the man to his feet with little effort. "And no more bowing."

Wang nearly bowed to acknowledge the order. He stopped himself, saying, "I will try to remember. But, Mr. Lang, what of the Emperor? You must return home!"

Bleak though he felt, Yi Xiao managed a smile, "Whatever happens in China is beyond our control. It has been more than three months since I left. It will take at least that long to return. By then, the Emperor's illness will have passed one way or another. A week, at most, will hardly affect matters. I have promised that child protection and I must and will keep that promise."

"I... yes... a Prince must keep his word. I see that."

Having won the argument, Yi Xiao continued. "I will remain at the inn with my companions. It would look strange for me to leave them. You may accompany me, if you must, but be careful to treat me as you would any other man." He'd make sure Jo was safely settled, preferably with some family who would love and care for her, then evade this man somewhere in America's mountains.

And, with luck, evade Gan Han as well.

ooo

It took two days to prepare for the trip to the mine. In that time Jo barely said more than a few words to Yi Xiao. He didn't seem to notice but he was expert at keeping his feelings to himself. Better at it than she was, certainly. But how was she supposed to feel, with him letting Burns walk all over her like that?

It was Hai Chan, who was getting ready to leave them for his newly acquired ship, who took her aside to talk. "I've been sailing long enough to know when something's brewing. What is it?"

"I have no idea what you mean."

"Yes, you do."

Hai Chan was one of those straightforward, no-nonsense sorts one couldn't lie to. Came to that, Jo doubted she could lie to Yi Xiao, but that was because the man would see through her. "I don't want to be doing this. Burns is a nasty, dirty, old scoundrel who doesn't deserve whatever my uncle left us."

"I can't blame you for not liking it," Hai Chan admitted. "But that's not why you're acting like Yi Xiao cut your anchor and sliced your sails for you."

Somewhere below them, Yi Xiao was practicing his dance again, performing for a half-dozen young women from the saloon down the street. They were applauding wildly and someone was playing a harmonica in time with his movements. That was part of the problem. She wanted him to ask why she was upset, so she could tell him off. But he either hadn't noticed or wouldn't admit it.

"He didn't have to treat me like a little kid."

That made Hai Chan laugh, which almost offended her all over again. "You are a child. So is Gan Han, for all she refuses to admit it."

"Still, that was my property he bargained with. He didn't ought to have lectured me on what's right and wrong. Not right in front of Burns like that."

Hai Chan leaned out the window and shouted to Yi Xiao, "Hey. Apologize to Jo!"

"All right." Yi Xiao clambered up the back wall of the inn and clung to the window sill. "Apologize for what?"

"Treating her like a baby and making her feel bad about not wanting to keep her father's bargain."

It startled Jo to realize just how precisely Hai Chan pinned down why she was angry. "You could at least have talked to me private-like. Made me feel stuck in a corner."

Yi Xiao thought on that a moment. "I too felt 'stuck in a corner'," he admitted. "Which, when you think about it, we were. Do you think Burns and his men would give up without a fight?"

"No." She'd expected a brawl and had been quite ready to give them what they asked for.

"Do you really, truly, believe we'd have won?"

"You could beat them. I've seen you fight." Admittedly, it'd mostly been him evading and blocking Gan Han whenever she tried to force him to draw his weapon. It was still obvious he knew what he was doing.

"Maybe. But why fight when you don't have to?" Jo's mother would have agreed. She was always on Jo to stop brawling with the neighbor boys. Seeing her begin to falter, Yi Xiao pressed his point. "Master says, violence is what happens when we forget the *Dao*."

"Your master sure did have a saying for everything," Jo muttered. She didn't understand Yi Xiao's *Dao* and didn't want to. Still, "I don't want to fight just to fight. It's just that Burns isn't...."

"Isn't a good man. I know. I don't like him or how he behaves either. But not liking a person doesn't give you carte blanche to break your word. Would you have changed your mind if I'd told you so in private?"

Jo thought on that a moment and sighed. She probably would have. The biggest reason she'd been annoyed had been looking at that smug smirk on Burns' face when Yi Xiao sided with him. "Yes."

"Then if there is another time when I must persuade you of a thing, I will try to do it without an audience."

She managed a smile. "All right. Now will you get back down from here before you break your neck?"

With a laugh, he flung himself backwards, putting her heart straight up her throat as he spun around and landed lightly on the pavement below. She didn't know if he could fight much, but he'd make some circus one heck of an acrobat.

Or, more likely, a clown.

OOO

They left Hai Chan behind in San Francisco, gathering a crew of disappointed prospectors. As he'd predicted, the Gold Rush had proved less than profitable for the vast majority of its fortune-hunters. Gold didn't pave the riverbeds nor glitter in every rock. Some more stubborn prospectors were sure they just had to find the right stream, explore the right mountain, and they'd be rich beyond their wildest dreams. Others just wanted to go home with enough profit to make the trip worth it.

Once they'd gathered supplies they headed north from San Francisco, crossing the bay by ferry and following a narrow, difficult, roadway into the hills. To Burns' disgust, they were forced to leave the horses and mule behind in Sausalito, carrying the heavy equipment themselves. He was equally disgusted when Gan Han insisted on coming along. "Girls don't belong on trips like this!"

Yi Xiao pointed out, "You don't object to Jo coming along."

"That's only 'cause she won't give me the map."

It was also because Yi Xiao wouldn't let him take the map, but neither man mentioned the point. "The camp we're headed for is only ten or so miles away. Master says, a little walk never hurt anybody."

Caleb Yancey's property might be only ten miles away from San Francisco, but it was ten miles of twists and turns and ups and downs, to the annoyance of everyone but Yi Xiao. It wasn't exactly the same as Heng Shan—the plants and wildlife were too different—but it still felt pleasantly familiar. He looked forward to exploring it further, once he was alone.

They were nearing their destination when shouts, clangs, and thuds echoed down the narrow valley. A fight, from the sound of it, and one with oddly familiar words. Yi Xiao couldn't be sure, but he thought he heard someone yelling in Hunanese about restoring something.

"Your Highness, I believe those are rebels. You should let me and my men go ahead."

"What's that friend of yours talking about, Chinaman? Tell him to talk English, stead of that gobbledygook."

"Should we hurry? That sounds like it's right near my Uncle's place!"

"It sounds like a fight. Would you like your sabre?"

Yi Xiao gazed through the trees, spotting smoke around the bend of the trail. "Master says, where there's smoke, there's fire." He returned his attention to his companions. "Wang, this is America. Chinese laws don't apply. Burns, not everything he says is about you. Jo, don't run straight into trouble. Gan Han. No. Just no."

Having made his position clear, Yi Xiao strode up the trail as quickly as his legs could carry him. The others followed, arguing with him and with each other, but he ignored their fuss in favor of the one ahead.

Rounding the corner, Yi Xiao took in the situation. A village of sorts had grown up beside the narrow stream leading down from the steep hillside. Composed mostly of small tents and a few wooden structures, it had a temporary air, made the more so by the fact that it was being torn apart by a large group of white men. This in spite of the dozen or so Chinese trying to stop them.

The central structure was the source of the smoke and Yi Xiao recognized a smithy in the midst of being burned down by a group of the attackers, to the fury of its obvious owner; a tall black man wielding a bar of iron as if it were bamboo. Already three of his attackers had gone down and he was working on the fourth. Not that his efforts were enough to protect his property. There were just too many enemies.

Not liking the odds, Yi Xiao started forward, only to find Wang holding him back. "I cannot allow you to endanger yourself."

"You don't have a choice," Yi Xiao told him, slipping his grip before the man had a chance to react. Wang's men tried to catch hold of him next, but by then Yi Xiao had rolled past them and was running up the path. Gan Han came up beside him, saying, "You don't even know why they're fighting."

She was right, of course, but from the look of the place, the white men were the intruders. While they might have the law behind them, he saw nothing suggesting it. "Don't kill anyone," he ordered her, catching hold of one of the men breaking down the smithy and tossing him into the nearby stream.

"I'm a swordswoman. I'm not trained to fight without killing."

"Start learning." Yi Xiao elbowed the next man in the chest, ducked beneath the smith's staff and kicked another man in the ear. "Or you'll be the next one I knock out."

"You will not." She swung around, knocking an attacker unconscious with a carefully controlled blow. Yi Xiao focused his attention on the men still trying to burn down the smithy. A pinpoint strike here, a kick there, an arm twist and a knee lock; all while trying to put out the fire with water from the dousing tank.

Wang and his men rushed into camp a minute later, forcing Yi Xiao to shout, "Don't kill anyone!" The order clearly confused his would-be defenders. Unlike Gan Han, they didn't argue, knocking men out as they spread through camp.

Within minutes the battle was over, with men lying on the ground groaning, or simply breathing heavily, staring at the sky. Yi Xiao set the last of his opponents down on the ground, patted his cheek, then turned to the smith. "Are you hurt?"

"Only a little.... you speak good English, mister. Who are you?"

"Your Highness, you are unhurt?" Wang demanded, rushing up to Yi Xiao.

"Don't call me that. Someone will understand you here," Yi Xiao told the man in Chinese, then turned his attention back to the smith, once again speaking in English. "My name is...."

"Your Highness?" The man's Chinese was as startlingly good as Yi Xiao knew his English was to most westerners. "You're a prince?"

"That's what he says," Yi Xiao sighed, supposing it only made sense for a man working with so many Chinese speakers to have learned the language. "I beg you not to mention it."

"I'm in your debt. I'll hold my tongue. Though I'm afraid your friend here might not."

As if to prove the point, Wang was busy scolding him, "You can't rush off into danger like that, your Highness! It's our job to defend you." His voice was loud and angry, loud enough to attract the unwelcome attention of the Chinese miners. They gathered close, their unfriendly expressions causing Wang's men to circle around Yi Xiao, guarding him from attack. A moment later Gan Han joined them, sword ready.

"Depose the Qing! Restore the Ming!" someone shouted angrily. As if to make things worse, Burns and his men hurried up the path, yelling something about claim-jumpers and squatters.

000

Jo had watched the fight from a safe spot on the hillside above, excitement setting her blood racing. Gan Han in particular, left her in awe. The Chinese woman's movements flowed from one position to the next, a rapid series of blows and kicks, combined with strikes with the flat of her blade that knocked her opponents out easily. Jo itched to join in, but knew she wasn't up to it.

Compared to Gan Han, Yi Xiao didn't seem nearly as good. He barely ever raised a fist, contenting himself with finger poking, swooping movements and foot sweeps. He didn't even take the offensive, staying close to the forge and occasionally throwing a bucket of water on the burning wall. Admittedly, the fire was important but Jo felt more admiration for Gan Han—who was all over the place with her attacks—than for Yi Xiao's cautious defense.

When the fight ended and the miners surrounded Yi Xiao, Jo thought they were going to thank him. Except someone was shouting in an unfriendly way, his voice drowned out a moment later by Burns and his men adding fuel to the fire by accusing the Chinese of claim jumping.

Jo should have stayed put but her impetuous nature set her running into the camp, pushing her way through to Yi Xiao and Gan Han. "Stop it!" she yelled, "He just helped you!" Belatedly it occurred to her that these men had no reason to listen to her. Worse, all she'd done was make herself a target. Another fight was brewing and she and her companions were at the center.

A clang loud as thunder broke through the noise. "ENOUGH!" As the crowd returned to shouting, the big blacksmith slammed his staff against his anvil again. "I SAID ENOUGH!"

The voice was familiar, even if the man's face hadn't been. It'd been six years since Jo's uncle had left home, with his best friend Zak for company. Caleb had planned on settling in Ohio but somehow wound up all the way out in California, working for Sutter. Zak must have stayed with him, though he'd obviously done some growing since then. He'd been a skinny fellow of fifteen the last time she'd seen him. His voice was the same, though, deep and resonant and able to shout the cows home from across the field.

That shout silenced everyone in the little settlement, too. Jo looked up at Zak, barely able to see the scrawny nervous youth she remembered in those broad shoulders and confident features. "Now then. I'm not sure what's going on, and I don't know who you lot are, but we've had enough fighting." He said something in Chinese that made the obvious leader of the miners frown. He was an older man, with a pinched up face and pursed lips that tightened every time he glanced at Yi Xiao.

"Zak? What's going on here?" Jo asked, eliciting a well-remembered smile. Zak used to carry her on his shoulders when she'd been little and she guessed he remembered her fondly enough.

"Little girl, you shouldn't be out here in the wild on your own. Where's your Pa?" Zak's voice faltered when he saw her face. "Oh. I see. We'll talk about it later, when things are quieter."

The miners' leader interrupted, speaking in English out of deference for Jo. "The child is safe but we will not allow a Prince of the Qing to stay among us."

Wang stepped towards the miner but Yi Xiao was in front of him and bowing politely before his self-appointed guard could say a word. Like the miner, he spoke in English. "Sir, I have no intent of interfering with you and your fellows. By the Mother of Lightning, I swear it."

"You dare swear by Her?"

Once again Zak put his staff down, the sound echoing up and down the valley. "We don't have much time. It's almost night and we have to get everyone in the shelter before it gets dark."

"Leave those thieves and these Manchu scum to the voice that calls in the night. You may bring the girls inside, if you want."

Zak snapped, "I don't know what your problem is with these people, but there's no way I'm agreeing to leaving anyone to that thing."

"He's one of our oppressors!"

"He isn't wrong," Yi Xiao admitted. "I am a Manchu, after all."

The statement didn't help at all and Jo snapped, "Why do you gotta be so much trouble? Can't you keep your mouth shut for nothing?" She didn't know what it was made Zak so nervous but he had a cool head on his shoulders. If he thought there was something bad coming, he was probably right.

Off to the side and sulking because he was being ignored, Burns suddenly snapped, "Where's that box your uncle left you, girl? The sooner I have what I came for, the sooner we can part ways."

Zak frowned on the man. "What are you talking about, mister?" He stopped himself, gesturing towards a solid barn. "No. Tell me later. Everyone, we have got to get inside. If you can walk, you grab someone who can't. And for your lives sake, don't call anyone by their name!" He turned a worried look on the sky. "Getting dark. Not much time left."

"How dare you tell me what to do?" Burns might have said more but Zak's commanding voice did its job. People were dragging the unconscious into the barn without argument.

Yi Xiao said something incomprehensible to Wang, who bristled. Except Yi Xiao's voice, usually soft and unassuming, held a note of command just like Zak's. Wang bowed, giving orders to the others and helping clear the campsite of the unconscious and injured.

Zak grinned at Yi Xiao. "Come on, your Highness. Get inside to safety. We can talk about it later."

ooo

They'd barely gotten a few feet into the surprisingly well-lit barn when Yi Xiao realized Burns and his men weren't coming. "Damn him, anyway," he muttered. He had no idea why Zak wanted everyone inside but he could tell the man was afraid. Zak didn't look the type to scare easily.

When Yi Xiao started back for the others, Zak put a hand on his shoulder. "Stay here. I know how to keep it off. You don't."

"It?"

"Yeah." The man glanced back outside. "I don't know what it is. Some hoodoo a fellow from the next mine camp over sent us. I've been fighting it off every dark moon for months now."

"Can you keep them safe as well as yourself?" Yi Xiao asked, pointing. Burns' men were following him towards an opening in the rocks on the other side of the settlement. He could hear Burns giving querulous orders as he went. "I don't believe they're going to cooperate."

Zak had the look of a man with a severe headache. "Where the hell do they think they're going?"

"Jo's father promised Burns something before he died. The Reverend is nothing if not persistent." Yi Xiao went outside, to Zak's obvious annoyance. "You said we have until nightfall? Perhaps we can persuade them to come inside before it gets dark."

"Doubt it, but we better try." Zak headed for the cave.

Yi Xiao followed behind. "What is this thing you fear?"

"I wish I knew. Wish we could leave. It's got our names, though, and it follows us wherever we go. Ah Sen made it all the way down to San Francisco before it found him." Zak stopped in his smithy to get a lantern. "It doesn't like fire, or light, so as long as the one it calls doesn't answer, it can't hurt anyone. Trouble is, it won't stop calling until morning. So I have to keep it distracted."

At a guess 'it' was some kind of monster, created by an unfortunate combination of human fears and the presence of strong magic. "What does it do to its victims?"

"We don't know. Them it takes, it takes away. All we ever find are bones, their marrow sucked dry." Zak clambered up the last rocks to the cave entrance. "It attacks with the ones it killed, but they're not strong. Just empty skin, mostly. And it doesn't know my real name cause I don't, so it can't call me proper."

That would be why Zak was the best one at the camp to fight the thing. "It doesn't know my name, either,"

"I hope you're right about that. If it does, you'll have a hard time ignoring it."

"Master says, don't borrow trouble when you're neck deep already," Yi Xiao answered, to Zak's great amusement. "Let's find those others and get out of here."

The inside of the cave was dry and dark. Its walls echoed every sound, a soft susurration that reminded Yi Xiao of the sort of voices one might hear falling asleep, when one's dreams tried to start too soon. Zak handed him the lantern. "Don't talk. The less attention you draw, the better."

The whispering became more like a voice, though still incomprehensible. Yi Xiao followed Zak as silently as he'd been ordered, scanning the dark grey stones and spotting tool marks and other signs of mining. The prospectors must have searched for gold here before. He yearned to ask questions but knew Zak was right.

Burns and his men weren't as sensible. They searched around somewhere ahead, muttering and talking to each other. Calling each other by name and entirely unaware of the whispers in the dark. Yi Xiao could hear the word 'hungry' in them, oddly enough in the Hunan dialect. Then Burns' name echoed and the man himself bleated like a terrified goat. Arriving just in time, Yi Xiao grabbed him by the shoulder, "All of you. Out of here!"

They ran willingly, the voice in the darkness more than they could take. Burns was the only one who didn't move, requiring both Zak and Yi Xiao to pull him along as fast as they could. They ran back outside, into the twilight, back across the stream and finally into the barn. All while something fluttered after them. What was it? Cloth? A swirl of dust covered cobwebs? An empty bag of human skin?

Burns struggled, trying to go back, screaming that he was being called. Yi Xiao struck Burns behind the ear, paralyzing him, then shoved the stiff body through the door to the barn. He turned and joined Zak in staring the monster down.

When it began chanting a new name, ice crawled straight up Yi Xiao's spine.

"Jo. Jo. Jo."

ooo

The miners tried to hold Jo back but she was fast and slippery, escaping outside before anyone could stop her. She knew the thing meant to eat her but she couldn't fight the urge to do what it wanted. She moved towards it, feeling its empty flesh grasp her outstretched arms. It was a filthy touch, dry and desiccated, like old and dusty parchment. She'd have screamed if it didn't have its claws in her head already.

Zak caught hold of her, dragging her backwards and trying to push her into the barn. She struggled to slip free, yearning to answer the call. Visions of her father, of her mother, of her little brother, all rose in her mind. She'd never have to grieve again. Oblivion would claim her and she'd be one with it. Just as the others were.

Something bright red fluttered into view. One of Yi Xiao's scarves, distracting Jo from her trance. "Your name's not Jo," he said. "You don't have to listen."

Jo was short for Josephine, but it was what everyone had called her for years. Of course it was her name. She struggled to break free of Zak's grip, to embrace nothing and forget everything. Except Yi Xiao wouldn't let her. He yelled something in Chinese and someone in the barn began striking the wall. It almost sounded like a heart beat and she felt her own heart pound to its rhythm.

At the same time Yi Xiao began spinning and dancing around the thing trying to consume her. A chill wind blew down the valley, damp and tingling like the air after a stroke of lightning. The emptied skin tried

"ALL OF YOU. OUT OF HERE!"

to slash at Yi Xiao, its substance catching at him. "Prince of Qing," it whispered and sounded desperate.

With the thing no longer focused on Jo, she found herself freed. She and Zak sprawled in the dirt. Realizing it'd turned its attention on Yi Xiao and knowing how hard it was to fight; Jo searched for a weapon and found it in the weapon Gan Han kept trying to give Yi Xiao. She yanked it from the dirt and tried to swing it, nearly cutting off her toes in the process.

At the same time Yi Xiao kept dancing, showing amazing focus given what the thing could do. Still, it was only a matter of time before its will overwhelmed his. Jo couldn't let that happen and she swung the blade again, cutting into the non-fabric and once again drawing its attention. It stretched an 'arm' out towards her, the shapeless mass becoming more real as it said her name.

Jo fought the urge to listen as Zak slammed his staff into the thing and flung it several yards away. It was up again a moment later, calling out, "Zak."

"Sorry. Not here."

The wind was getting stronger and now it was beginning to spark, as if a small thunderstorm was forming. It followed Yi Xiao, who spun around and around as if he were at the center of a twister. The wind dragged the thing along, catching hold of its 'substance' and spinning it.

Yi Xiao dropped to one knee below the whirlwind. Jo caught sight of his face and almost dropped his blade. The kindly, humorous, man she was so fond of had disappeared, lost behind a demonic mask of bloodlust and killing intent. She fell backwards, staring wildly at her friend. "...no...."

Something flickered in Yi Xiao's eyes and was gone. As the thing reached for him, he wrapped his scarf around its outstretched wrist. Once again it whispered, desperately. "Prince of Qing!"

"No," Yi Xiao said firmly. "I am not." Then he gestured and the wind dove straight into the flames of Zak's smithy, until the storm was terrifying mixture of mist, dead branches and fire. Something screamed at its center as the whole mess shrank in on itself and disappeared.

For a moment Jo couldn't find a single word to say. She stared at Yi Xiao as his expression softened, returning to the old, gentle, one Jo was accustomed to. Slowly, she stammered, "What are you? What kind of hoodoo are you?"

"I don't even know what that is," he complained, spreading his hands as if that would prove he was harmless. "But I can guess. It wasn't magic. Not quite."

The fear in Jo's eyes must have been obvious, for he sighed. "I see. Well, I'll be on my way then." When she didn't argue, he turned away, adding, "For what it's worth, I'm glad you're safe. Zak, don't let that Burns fellow walk all over her."

"I won't. I don't understand what's going on, but I won't."

"Jo, be careful with that sabre. Make Gan Han show you how to use it, if you insist on swinging it around." Jo's silence made him sigh. He walked away into the shadows but his voice echoed back to them. "I'm so tired of killing. I'm glad nothing died, this time."

Then he was gone.

Chapter 5: Earth –
An Encouraging Resolution

The next few days were occupied in cleaning up the mess from the fight. As the settlement's owner, Zak Striker spent most of it getting the claim-jumpers down to Sausalito. He held little hope his prisoners would be punished for attacking his mine camp. Chinese miners were mostly admired for their hard-working ethos and sober ways, but they weren't citizens and they weren't white. The law didn't favor them any more than it favored a free man of color like Zak.

Jo came along on the trip and she talked his ear off the whole way. By the time they reached Sausalito, Zak knew all there was to know about her journeys and how her Pa had died trying to protect her. The only thing she didn't talk about was the odd Chinese man who'd brought her to camp; nor even how she'd come to travel with him.

Zak wasn't sure who she was madder at; her friend or herself. She always did have a short temper, though, and Yi Xiao had scared her badly. After years of traveling with Caleb and running into the occasional odd occurrence, Zak was less bothered. He knew enough about magic to understand that it was the user who decided how to wield it.

The miners who helped him with the prisoners were more vocal about the stranger. The young man was obviously one of the Emperor of China's many sons. A soldier of Wang's high rank would never be assigned to protect anyone less important. And that, in turn, made him an enemy to any right thinking Han like themselves.

Zak didn't argue the point. He'd listened to his leasees' long and bitter discussions of the cruelties of the Manchu for months now. He even sympathized with them. But if Yi Xiao really was an Imperial Prince he seemed a harmless, kind, and sensible sort; hardly the tyrant his rebellious subjects claimed. Besides, if Yi Xiao were the prince then why hadn't that thing been able to call him? Zak had the advantage of having forgotten his real name years ago. Yi Xiao surely knew whether or not the title Prince belonged to him.

Admittedly, a title alone might not be enough, but that thing only needed part of a person's name to work. Yi Xiao hadn't even flinched when it'd called him. That hoodoo of his might have protected him, but Zak doubted it. It made him curious to know just who and what Yi Xiao was. Not that he was likely to find out anytime soon, given Yi Xiao had run off.

When they returned to the camp it was to find Reverend Burns and his men guarding the safe Zak and Caleb kept in the storage cave. The rest of the miners were guarding them, keeping them from getting into the rusty old thing. Near as Zak could tell, it was a stand-off that'd been going on a while. Burns and his men looked like they hadn't slept a wink for days.

"Jo told me what you're here for," Zak told Burns before the man could open his mouth. "So I understand you got some right to what's in that safe. But you don't got right to all of it."

Burns didn't like a black man telling him what to do but at least he didn't argue the point. Maybe he was too tired. "I didn't plan on taking everything. Just what was promised me."

"That'd be the agreement Hal had with you for helping Jo out, right?" Behind Zak, Jo muttered angrily, still hot over the whole thing.

"Exactly."

"Well now, I can't argue with that." Zak opened the safe and pulled out the two folders sitting inside. "See, back when Caleb sent that letter to Hal, he'd used his share of our profits to buy the valley over that ridge there. He figured Hal could come out, run it like he and I were running this one. These are the deeds to that valley and this."

Greed glittered in Burns' eyes. "What's this valley worth?"

Zak grinned. "Oh, nothing to you, cause when Caleb died, he willed his share to me. I was his partner after all. And before you ask how a slave can own a damned thing, I'll point out I'm a free man and a born citizen of these United States. So the law's on my side."

Burns might have argued the point but he remembered the miners surrounding them and he backed down quick. "And the other?"

"Like I said, it's right next door, so likely it's got as good a source of gold as we have. You'll have to go downhill a piece to get over to it, but it'd be yours all free and clear." Jo bristled a little at the suggestion but Zak ignored her. He and his miners could have got rid of Burns and his men easy, but he didn't want the sort of trouble killing someone could bring. Not to mention it just wasn't right.

It only took Burns a moment to make up his mind. "Fine. I'll take that valley." He snatched the folder and had his men packing to head out before anyone could say another word.

Given how annoyed she was, it was a miracle Jo kept her mouth shut until her nemesis had gone. "I hate this. He took advantage of my Pa, saving my life. He don't deserve no fortune."

Zak was tempted to correct her grammar but knew from experience she wouldn't listen. "You're right. He doesn't deserve it. But maybe he deserves what he's going to get." He jerked his thumb over his shoulder towards the hillside. "Those men we just dropped off at the Sausalito jail? They were claim jumpers who took over that valley after your uncle died. I've been trying to pry them out ever since." Jo stared and smiled broadly. "Reverend Burns and his friends can have the joy of trying, now, and you can have half this valley instead. Just like Caleb would have wanted."

Now Jo looked really pleased as she flung her arms around Zak and crowed. "Thank you! I'm going to go tell Gan Han!"

Ma Yun, the miner's headman and spokesperson, interrupted. "The young lady's gone, just like those other bastards. I think they went after that Prince of theirs. Good riddance."

Somehow Zak had a feeling Yi Xiao wouldn't be nearly so pleased.

ooo

For the first time since he'd left Heng Shan, Yi Xiao was alone and surrounded by nothing but trees, bushes, rocks and water. Everything was different, but in essence, everything was the same. It wasn't home, but he could make a life here and be content. Or he could, if he weren't so disquieted by everything that had led him to this place.

Thinking about it, he'd let himself get too attached to the girl. Back on Heng Shan he'd always known he could see his family any time. It'd given him a solid base, a feeling of connection to the world. Here in America, with no way to tell if his family was safe and no way to return to them quickly, he'd felt lost. Jo, so like his young half-sister, had been an anchor in this strange land. Even her annoyance with him, when he'd made her angry for scolding her in public, had felt familiar, normal and right.

The fight with nothingness had changed their relationship. Yi Jin would never be terrified of him. She'd seen him at his worst, when the killing urge was on him and only their father's restraint could hold him back. Jo, having never seen such powers in her life, having never seen the light of violence in his eyes before, had wanted him gone and out of sight. It hurt in a way he hadn't expected. Even understanding the reason for her fear didn't help him feel better. He needed time and quiet to think.

The remarkably huge trees of California's coast provided Yi Xiao with a place to hide. His woodcraft provided him with nourishment. His training provided him with the beginnings of emotional replenishment. What none of those things could do was keep him from being bothered.

One problem was Gan Han. The young lady was obstinate and despite her complete lack of woodcraft, somehow able to follow him. It took him several days of constantly having to change his campsite before he realized it was his sabre—once more in her hands—that betrayed him.

It was mere metal, a particularly fine blade handed down through the Lang family's line from an illustrious ancestress. Yet in Gan Han's hands, it was a tie to him that let her search him out. He wondered if she knew she possessed such a talent and guessed she'd never believe him if he tried to tell her.

Then there was Wang, who didn't need Yi Xiao's sabre to follow him. Instead the soldier trailed after Gan Han, despite her attempts to lose him. Yi Xiao could hide his presence and cover his tracks all he wanted but he couldn't hide hers.

On leaving the mining camp, Yi Xiao climbed up and down the hills surrounding the area. He wasn't sure why, but something held him there, a sense of unfinished business with Jo and the others. Yet at the same time he had no reason to approach and plenty of reason to avoid.

About a week later, Yi Xiao climbed to the top of the tallest mountain in the area. It was steep and difficult for someone unaccustomed to such things like Gan Han and Wang. It also afforded him both a grand view and a place to seek focus until his pursuit caught up again. He didn't doubt they would, but it'd take them some time to get there. He'd led them on a merry chase some miles north before heading south again. Besides, while the mountain was no steeper than Heng Shan, it lacked steps. They'd have to crawl their way up the rocks.

Like Heng Shan, the mountain was one of those places with deep roots into the world; a holy place, sacred to those who knew such things. It was a good place, a balanced place, and one where Yi Xiao could cultivate his *qi* and replenish his Self. A place where he could come to terms with what disturbed him and why. As he understood why Jo's reaction had hurt, he also understood it didn't matter. Not really.

Yi Xiao had been so caught up in his childish reaction to Jo's fear he hadn't recognized his real accomplishments. He'd mastered his inner strength, so that his *qi* attack barely tired him. He'd mastered his killing desire against the men he'd fought. He'd mastered his Self, maintaining balance against a force that meant to obliterate him.

Even better, Yi Xiao had done all this without killing. The thing he'd fought had been a mental construct, a *tulpa* formed from a dead man's life force. What little remained of the soul used to create it could only be freed, not saved. As for its master, well they'd have a headache for awhile but nothing worse.

By late afternoon, something roused Yi Xiao. Gan Han? Wang and his men? No, it couldn't be. They'd be coming after him from the mountain's northern side. This movement came from the south, a sound of rustling in the bushes below.

Lying on his belly, Yi Xiao peered over the edge. Two men were climbing towards him. They were too busy to look up, but Yi Xiao thought they were familiar. That was right, he'd knocked the one on the left unconscious at Zak's smithy a week ago.

Under other circumstances Yi Xiao might have hailed the strangers and asked them what they were doing. Not wanting attention, however, he slid backwards to hide in the nearest bushes. Unlike the approaching pair, he could be as silent as a breeze.

The men weren't trying to hide. They grumbled under their breath, complaining about the steep hill, the loose rocks and the fact that they were there at all. "Don't know why we both had to come."

"To keep the other honest," the second man suggested.

"Hah!"

"All right, honest ain't the word. But if one of us has to piss, the other can keep watching." The man cursed as he stuck his hand in some thorns. "Won't be long, anyway. Just gotta wait until it starts getting dark. Soon as those Chinee and that black bastard settle down for the night, we'll give the signal."

Yi Xiao realized these men planned another attack on Zak's mine camp. Though he wasn't sure he wanted to deal with Jo's fears, or his countrymen's hatred, he also didn't want anyone hurt. No one had died in the last attack but that had been sheer good fortune. They might not be so lucky next time.

Silently, Yi Xiao headed back to the camp. It was only a mile or so away, but steep and difficult as the mountains were, it would still take him at least an hour or so to get there.

∞∞

It was late afternoon when Zak heard angry curses outside his smithy. Sighing, because sometimes it seemed like the bunch he'd leased the mine to were incapable of going a day without an argument, he set his hammer down and stepped outside.

This time the men had reason, though he still wasn't sure it was a good one. The young man sauntering up the trail towards camp might be hoodoo and might be their oppressors' prince, but he'd done nothing to harm anyone in camp and quite a bit to help. Besides, Zak found it hard to dislike that friendly smile and easy-going personality. "Stop yelling," he ordered the men, knowing they wouldn't. At the same time he put himself between Yi Xiao and the others. "Afternoon, Yi Xiao. Or should I say, your Highness?"

"Yi Xiao is just fine, Zak. Despite Wang's insistence to the contrary, I'm not a Prince of any sort." Yi Xiao craned his neck so he could look past Zak, adding in Chinese, "I'm the Duke of Jin's youngest son and I promise, I don't care at all that you're members of the Heaven and Earth Society."

Zak was usually glad he'd taken the time to learn Chinese, but he would have felt more comfortable not understanding the threats and jeers the young man's assurance received. "I have no problem with you myself," he told Yi Xiao. "But they do. I'm not sure it's a good idea for you to stay."

The sound of something breaking interrupted the argument. Looking over, Zak saw Jo standing at her cabin door, the bowl she'd been drying smashed at her feet. She stared wild-eyed at Yi Xiao, then stepped back and slammed the door shut behind her, the faint sound of sobbing just audible.

"Was it something I said?" Before Zak could react to the man's idiocy, Yi Xiao added, "Tell her I'm sorry I scare her, would you? That was never my intent, but I know that doesn't change her feelings. Master says, apologies don't fix broken statues."

Somehow Zak suspected Yi Xiao had earned that particular lecture.

He didn't say so, returning his attention to the men surrounding them. "Will the lot of you please stop shouting?" To his surprise, they did, though their muttered imprecations weren't much better. "I hate to be inhospitable, but...."

"But you don't want another fight." Yi Xiao pointed off towards the peak of Mount Tam. "I wasn't hoping to stay. But I was just up there and overheard a couple of men spying on your camp. I have reason to believe they intend to attack you tonight."

"Liar!" That was Chao, youngest son of the miners' headman, Ma. Impetuous, thoughtless and given to getting into fights at the least opportunity, he was—naturally—the one most willing to go after a man who'd amply demonstrated an ability to command the wind. "You're just here to spy on us yourself!"

"I promise you that isn't true. I realize you have little reason to believe me, but I did see those men and hear their plan. When night falls and you settle in for bed, I fear they'll invade the camp and cut your throats in your sleep."

Chao swung his fist, striking Yi Xiao in the chin and knocking his head sideways, splitting the man's lip.

Instead of fighting back, Yi Xiao wiped the blood away. "I usually charge for any blow that lands." he told the other boy. "But in this case, I think I'll waive the fee. Besides, I have a proposal."

Chao's father grabbed his son's arm, holding him tight where he stood. "What?"

"I am the Storm Hermit's best—all right, her only—pupil. I will fight anyone you choose to a knockdown. If I win, you listen to what I've said and prepare yourself for your attackers. If I lose, I leave quietly and without argument."

Zak couldn't help interrupting. "I know these men pretty well. None of them have any hoodoo like yours."

Yi Xiao smiled, spreading his hands apologetically. "Despite appearances, *qi* is not magic. It is, however, an unfair advantage that I will not use as long as no one else here does."

The implication that one of the miners might have such a skill was obvious. If so, no one admitted it. Seeing Ma Yun appeared amenable, Zak sighed. "I won't argue then. But one knockdown and no serious injuries, understood?"

Both men bowed in agreement.

ooo

Yi Xiao borrowed a strip of cloth from one of the miners and tied it round his head. "I was required to cut my hair recently," he told Ma when the headman raised a curious brow. "It bothers me when I fight."

"Cut? Or grew it out?" Ma went to the center of the ring, swinging his queue around his neck to get it out of the way.

"I told you, I'm a disciple of the Storm Hermit and a follower of the *Dao*. Thus, I don't shave my forehead."

Although Ma snorted irritably at the claim, all he did was bow. Yi Xiao followed suit, then took up stance; left heel raised, right foot flat and turned sideways, hands spread in the wind dancing posture. "Any time you're ready."

Ma eyed Yi Xiao's stance critically. "Who taught you how to do that?"

"I told you, the Storm Hermit."

"That's not the right position for crane style."

"It's not crane style."

"Then what is it? Because you're off balance."

"I'm not supposed to be balanced."

"Who was the idiot taught you that?"

"If you want to call the Storm Hermit an idiot, go ahead. I, personally, wouldn't suggest it."

"You are such a liar. The Storm Hermit doesn't take pupils. And if she did, why the hell would she teach you such an unbalanced stance?"

"Master says, balance is in the mind. Achieve it there, and all else will follow."

From somewhere towards the back of the crowd, someone shouted, "Would you finish him already!"

"I just want to know what this young idiot is thinking. Manchus aren't usually this stupid and that stance...." Ma's sentence, suggesting he was entirely focused on the argument, broke off suddenly as he swung into action, taking two long steps forward, aiming his fist for Yi Xiao's chest.

Yi Xiao didn't give Ma time to reach him. He spun around, movement forcing his opponent to step further in than he would have otherwise. Before Ma recovered, Yi Xiao flung himself upwards and forward, somersaulting through the air, using the force of the motion to kick Ma in the ear and send him flying.

It almost worked. Ma hadn't expected the attack and barely managed to recover. He stumbled and forced himself upright. Then he launched a series of attacks—leopard style—that Yi Xiao countered with falling blossoms, blocking and redirecting the strikes.

Still, Ma managed to get a good solid hit in, sending Yi Xiao stumbling backwards. This time it was he who had to recover, dropping into a long, lightning strike, stance. They stared at each other for what seemed forever but really couldn't be more than a second or so. "Fast," Ma said. "Faster than I expected. You had good teachers, Prince."

"I have an excellent teacher and I'm not a prince," Yi Xiao answered, dodging beneath the man's next attack. Ma caught him by the shirt; fingers crooked in eagle claw, then shoved him between the shoulder blades, forcing him into a forward roll. He rose to his feet and turned to face the man, once more in wind dancing posture.

"The Americans have a saying. Fool me once, shame on you. Fool me twice, shame on me." Ma rushed him again, but this time spun into a position to block Yi Xiao's flying kick. When Yi Xiao landed and repeated the stance, the man shook his head. "Is that all you have? Don't keep doing the same...."

This time it was Yi Xiao who took advantage of the distraction, flinging himself forward in a roll that brought him right in front of Ma and kicking the man in the gut. It wasn't enough. Ma had a solid stance and Yi Xiao wasn't in the right position to put him off balance. Still, it was enough to make the man cough, which felt like an accomplishment.

Once more on his feet, Yi Xiao noticed a draft. Ma's eagle claw had done more than he'd realized. His cotton shirt was torn, the shoulder ripped down his back all the way to his belt. "I hope someone has a spare," he said. "Because I don't."

Ma didn't pay attention. He frowned at something behind Yi Xiao. "Turn around."

"Eh?"

"I said, turn around."

Ordinarily, Yi Xiao would never have obeyed such a command from an opponent but some instinct told him to do so now. He turned and saw the wide eyes of the audience behind him, their fingers jabbing and pointing as if he'd grown wings.

"Who are you?" Ma demanded suddenly. "The Mother of Lightning would never bless a Prince of the Qing."

Yi Xiao returned his attention to Ma. "I'm not a Prince."

"You're a Manchu of the royal house, yet you wear Her mark. Who. Are. You."

Yi Xiao glanced at his shoulder at the tiny lines—like dozens of lightning bolts—engraved on his flesh from wrist to shoulder and down his back. Inflicted by the Storm Hermit during his training, they were proof of his mastery of grounding. No one could survive her lightning without it.

The headman was waiting for Yi Xiao's answer impatiently. "I told you I'm the Storm Hermit's disciple."

"And I told you...." Ma stopped himself. "You're not who we thought. Please, sir. Tell us who you really are?"

"Lang Yi Xiao, the Wanderer. Least worthy and youngest son of the House of the White Wolf. And," he added more brightly, "not at all interested in fighting rebels, if they aren't interested in fighting me."

While the miners checked the borders of the camp and set up traps for the would-be claim jumpers, Zak went to find Jo. He'd been so caught up in dealing with Yi Xiao he'd half-forgotten how upset she was by the young man's presence. Fortunately, despite having gone to hide, she was easily found. She'd always liked caves and the one right near the campsite was a favorite place for her.

"I'm glad you didn't go deeper," Zak remarked, shining his lantern around. The cave had been his and Caleb's first dig, a straight tunnel going through the southwestern ridge of the valley wall. They'd found a little gold before a fault in the stone made it too dangerous to mine. In the end, they'd blocked the far end and made the cave a storage room.

Jo sat in a corner with a candle, knees pulled to her chest and arms wrapped round tight like she was still the little girl who got picked on by the bigger kids. She'd always given as good as she got, but her ma's scolding would have her sulking for days. "Is he gone?"

"No, and he's not going to leave." Zak sat beside her. "He's not a bad sort."

To his surprise, she burst into tears. "I KNOW!"

Now Zak really didn't understand. "If you know, why are you hiding from him?"

"I was scared of him. I was traveling with him for weeks. I knew he was dangerous, but I knew he was trying hard not to be. How can I be looking him in the eyes now?"

"He said to tell you he's sorry about that." Zak didn't know what *qi* was, nor if Yi Xiao was right about it not being magic, but he did know it was powerful. "You had good reason to be. The sort of thing he did isn't natural."

"You're not scared of it," Jo pointed out, wiping tears from her face and smearing dust all over.

"I've seen enough hoodoo, traveling with Caleb to know it's not the power you should be scared of, it's the person using it."

Jo shuddered suddenly. "You didn't see his eyes that night. He had the killing urge on him something fierce."

"I saw it when he was fighting those bastards earlier," Zak pointed out. "Not a single one died, even though some of them gave him cause." It'd been a terrifying sight, the fierce, joyful, expression of glee, combined with near perfect control. The same look had flickered in Yi Xiao's eyes during the duel. Zak didn't know how Ma—seeing that expression—had managed to keep from running in terror.

A thought occurred to Jo and she looked sad. "That's what he's been dealing with, this whole time, I bet. He told Gan Han he doesn't want to kill anymore, a while back. Didn't occur to me that meant he had to have, at least once." She smiled, a little weakly. "I trusted him to get me this far and the only one got hurt was the one killed Pa. So I guess I can trust him not to hurt me now."

"Then let's go...." Zak rose, about to offer her his hand, when an explosion rocked the cave. "The hell was that? It's too late to be mining right now!" Besides, the miners had just found a nice little vein further into the valley. They didn't need to break any more rock yet.

Something cracked above them and Zak realized their danger just barely in time. "The roof's collapsing," he shouted, grabbing Jo's hand. "Run!"

OOO

The camp was just pretending to settle for the night when the explosion struck somewhere further up the valley. Startled voices began babbling immediately and Yi Xiao caught a whiff of gunpowder on the breeze. Stones rolled down the valley's southern ridge and a sound, like ice cracking, filled the air. As a cloud of dust and dirt spurted from the storage cave, Yi Xiao set off running.

Two figures stumbled out from amid the flying dust, coughing and choking. "Zak? Jo?" Relief was almost painful. "Are you hurt?"

"Naw," Jo managed. "Got out in time. What happened?"

It was Ma, coming up to join them, who answered. "Some fool set off an explosive further up the valley. I wouldn't be surprised if it were in the new mine shaft."

" HE SHOUTED, RUN ! "

Yi Xiao didn't understand. "Why would you blow up your mine shaft?" Realizing they were staring at him like a fool, he thought harder. "You mean sabotage, don't you?"

"Exactly." Zak wiped dirt from his face and glared up the valley. "I should have thought of it. Those men haven't been able to beat us up into going. That thing couldn't chase us out. The only way left is destroying our mine so we can't work."

Whomever was behind the attacks wouldn't be able to work a destroyed mine either, but Yi Xiao suspected the attacker hadn't thought of that. "Should we investigate?" Belatedly he realized he was including himself in the situation, despite not being involved.

Zak didn't comment on Yi Xiao's self-invitation. "We should. Jo, you stay here. If there's trouble I want you out of it."

"But...."

"You aren't big enough to do much damage. And before you point out that you shoot pretty good, I remind you that you've never had to kill a man. Besides, I'd like to avoid killing anyone. There's too much risk the law won't side with us." He squeezed her shoulder to comfort her. "You stay here and keep an eye on the camp in case those bastards come over for another round."

Jo sulked but accepted Zak's order. "All right. I won't let any of those yellow-bellied sapsuckers get in." She hesitated, looking shyly at Yi Xiao. "Sorry I was scared of you. Thanks for helping us now."

"I was frightening," Yi Xiao told her as Zak gathered a few men together. "I am frightening. I walked away from the martial world because I didn't want to be frightening."

She grinned at him and if her smile wasn't quite as full as it was before she'd seen his inner beast, it was bright enough to make him feel better.

ooo

The mine was at the far end of the valley, almost to the top of the long north-south ridge it descended from. They'd have built the camp closer, but the surrounding hillsides were too steep. Zak wondered if he should have had a guard staying up there anyway. It wasn't easy to reach, but a sufficiently determined climber could get anywhere.

It was almost dark by the time they neared the mine entrance. Their lanterns shone on freshly shattered rock and fallen trees, revealing someone had, indeed, set off an explosive. It was going to be one hell of a time clearing. Weeks, possibly months, depending on how deep the explosives had been when they'd gone off.

Zak's curses cut off when another, smaller, explosion split the air. Someone was shooting at them. "Cover your lanterns!" he shouted, concealing himself among the rocks. He scanned the cliffs above them but it was too dark to see anything but shadows.

Chao shouted, "I see them!" The impetuous young idiot immediately began scrambling up the side of the hill, making so much noise that—if there'd been a gunman on the other side—he'd have made a perfect target.

"Damnit, boy! Get back down here!" That was Ma, hiding near Zak. "Don't be a fool!"

Something shifted above Zak. Yi Xiao, using the cover of Chao's noise to climb the cliff-face. He was good, sure and steady. Zak just hoped he was also fast because he was certain the gunman wasn't alone. He'd heard more than one shot at one time.

With little else to do, Zak began herding his people back down the valley. Ma continued shouting at his son. Chao continued ignoring him. The others continued escaping, knowing better than to hang around. One by one, they ran from rock to rock as more bullets zinged past them. Until the only ones left were Ma, Chao, Zak and Yi Xiao.

"Damned if I'm going to leave it all up to those two," Zak muttered to Ma. "You keep yelling; it'll help distract those bastards. I'm going to try something."

Ma had no trouble shouting at his son. He'd spent most of the boy's life doing so, after all. Not that it did any good. Chao was and remained stubborner than the camp mule and just as hard headed. Of course, he came by it honestly, because Ma was just as bad if not worse.

Leaving Ma to entertain himself, Zak slipped further forward, closer to the shattered mine entrance. In the near total darkness, lit only by the waxing moon's light, he could barely see how the rocks had fallen in, creating a dangerously steep path. It'd be risky, but easier than the ways Chao and Yi Xiao had taken.

Zak soon discovered the flaw in his plan. The rocks weren't just steep, they were unstable. Not impossibly so, but he pinched his fingers and trapped his toes several times as he struggled to get up the slope. If Ma weren't shouting, the noise Zak made would have been easily noticed. Worse, he'd have been a sitting target for whoever it was up there.

By the time Zak reached the top, Chao was already there, crashing through the bushes and trees, searching for the gunmen. Not that he was having much success. It was too dark for such nonsense. Of course, Chao, convinced of his immortality, didn't seem to care.

Something flickered in Zak's vision. A crackle of lightning? Was a storm coming? Then he remembered Yi Xiao's strange hoodoo and realized the man had his own solution to the darkness. It was a dim light, hardly more than static electricity, but it was enough to draw a gunman's attention and make him fire in that direction.

Another flare—several feet away from the first—followed and another shot rang out. Again and again the gunmen tried to hit their constantly moving target and again and again they missed. Between Chao's noise and Yi Xiao's trickery, the enemy was running out of bullets. Even better, every time the men fired they revealed their positions. There were three of them, spread out among the trees.

Zak grinned, creeping through the darkness until he was just behind the closest of the three. He tapped the man on the shoulder, startling him into turning, then hit him in the jaw as hard as possible. Another thud followed soon after, as Yi Xiao knocked out the second man. As for the third, quieter and less given to firing blindly, sheer dumb luck turned in Chao's favor. The boy tripped over him and managed to knock him out after a brief struggle.

Once he'd tied the men with their own belts, Zak leaned over the cliff and called out, "Hey, Mr. Ma. Could you tell cook we'll have three for dinner?"

Ma went silent a moment. Then, "How would you prefer them? Stewed or fried?"

ooo

The men they'd captured were familiar yet unexpected. Yi Xiao had thought they'd be more claim jumpers. He hadn't anticipated their being Burns' men. When he commented on the fact, Zak coughed in an embarrassed way. "That Burns fellow wanted what Jo's Pa promised him; the deed to the valley over that ridge. I figured he and those claim-jumpers would fight over it and maybe solve our problems for us. Guess I figured wrong."

"Guess you did," Yi Xiao agreed wryly. "Though I'd have done the same. Burns is the sort who wants to be in charge. I have a feeling your claim-jumpers' leader is probably just as bad."

"I've never met him," Zak admitted. "Though I've tried. I'm told he doesn't like the color of my skin."

Yi Xiao had known Manchu like that, all too willing to abuse their Han subjects and all too sure of their superiority. He didn't say as much. He didn't know enough about the situation to comment. Besides, the man he was carrying was trying to talk. "Yes? Hello? Did you have something to say?"

The man's words were muffled, but he managed to make himself clear. "Burns is dead. Doc Jeffreys is in charge now."

"That'd be the boss of those claim-jumpers," Zak explained. "Sounds like he won the argument. I suppose I should have expected this sooner or later. So he killed your boss and you just fell over and joined him?"

Yi Xiao's captive growled under his breath. "That Doc Jeffreys is a hoo-doo man. He didn't just kill Burns, he turned him into a ghost. We don't do as he says; he'll do the same to us."

Hoodoo was the term Zak had used for magic. "A sorcerer? A necro-mancer?" It made a chilling sort of sense. The thing Yi Xiao had fought the other day had clearly been a necromantic summoning. "That... isn't good."

"Now that's an understatement if ever I heard one. I should have ex-pected something like this." Zak sounded exhausted and small blame to him. He and his fellow miners had no idea how to deal with a man like Jeffreys. "I don't suppose you...."

"I'm not a sorcerer," Yi Xiao pointed out. "What I do uses *qi*, not magic."

"From where I'm sitting, I don't see much difference."

Thinking on it, Yi Xiao supposed it would seem that way to an outsider. "Magic draws on energies from outside the world. *qi* on the energies from within. A really good, really powerful, sorcerer can stretch their influence for miles. I'm told the best a *qi* master can manage is an acre or so." There were other sources of power, some less influential, some so vast only the Gods could handle them. None of which mattered right then.

"Point is, can you do something to stop Jeffreys?"

"I don't know. I can destroy his creations, the same way I did the other, but stopping him? That probably means killing and I'm done with that. At least I want to be."

By this time they were getting close to the campsite and Yi Xiao slowed to a halt. "Didn't you post a guard?"

"I did."

Someone hissed at them from the trees. Jo. "Douse your lantern. Quick."

They didn't argue with her, though Chao might have. Fortunately, Ma put a hand over the boy's mouth and muttered, "For once in your life be quiet." To Yi Xiao's amazement, Chao obeyed, albeit sulkily.

In the meantime Jo slipped down the hillside quietly and told Zak, "We got trouble."

She didn't have to say more because they were close enough to the camp for Yi Xiao to hear raised voices. Some were yelling in Chinese, others in English, still others in Manchurian. He sighed. He'd expected Jeffreys. He'd expected Wang. He'd expected Gan Han. He hadn't expected them all at the same time.

ooo

Leaving their captives tied up behind them, with Ma and Chao to keep guard, Zak, Yi Xiao and Jo climbed up the slope of the valley. Zak wanted to leave Jo behind but could see by her expression that she wasn't going to cooperate. They didn't have time to argue the point, forcing him to agree.

"Don't expect me to rescue you if you get caught." Yi Xiao's callous statement made Zak bristle, until he added, "You're too smart to be a hostage, Jo. Find a way to get out of any trouble yourself."

The compliment was surprisingly effective. Zak supposed Jo must have been feeling useless for a while now. He hadn't helped, leaving her behind. But it was a good thing he had. She was the only one small and fast enough to slip off and warn them of the trouble ahead.

By now they'd reached a spot overlooking the campsite, where they could see everything going on clearly. Zak's understanding of Chinese was being tested, though some of what the miners were saying didn't need translation. Their meaning, vulgar and unrepeatable in polite company, was clear. Their sentiment was shared by the other two groups, creating an incomprehensible and slowly loudening babble of rage.

"Blood's gonna spill any minute," Zak muttered. "Can you do anything about your men, Yi Xiao?"

"Strictly speaking, they aren't mine. But since they think they are, maybe?" Yi Xiao scanned the scene and pointed, "The real problem's right there."

The man Yi Xiao pointed to was a tall, thin and elegantly dressed white man. He was watching the argument without expression, one hand clenched on a cane of what looked like carved bones. It was impossible to tell much about him but Zak guessed he was probably that Doc Jeffreys their captive had mentioned. He didn't look like much, but if he really had summoned the bone marrow eater he wasn't one Zak wanted to cross. Not that they had much choice.

Yi Xiao was already heading for the camp, sidling down the hillside in that slippery way of his. Zak stumbled after, with Jo a little bit behind. She was showing sense for once, understanding that she'd be putting him and Yi Xiao at risk if she got herself caught.

Zak got to the bottom of the hill just as Yi Xiao reached the soldiers who'd accompanied him earlier. As if to prove they considered themselves his, whether or not he agreed, they fell silent at his touch. Parting like the Red Sea, they let the young man pass without argument. Zak, arriving a moment or so later, hurried after, not wanting to get left behind.

The center of the argument was Yi Xiao's follower, the girl called Gan Han. Jo had told Zak she thought the girl was in love with Yi Xiao but the look she now turned on the young man held nothing but anger and distaste. Love could blossom in the strangest places but Zak doubted Jo's judgment. Such emotions weren't good soil for a long and happy relationship.

Jo came up behind Zak, staying close and keeping an eye behind them. "Gan Han? Why are they all yelling at her?"

"I don't think it's her they're mad at," Zak answered. "She's just put herself at the center of attention." Near as he could make out from the noise, Gan Han had decided to defend the miners against both Wang and Jeffreys. The latter's men didn't want to raise a hand to her because she was a girl. As for the former, he wasn't ready to risk her sword.

When Wang saw Yi Xiao he bowed and said something in a language Zak didn't know at all. Fortunately, Yi Xiao ordered, "Speak English. We're guests in this land and I don't want to have to translate for you."

"Lord, this girl defends the rebels. We meant to take them prisoner and return them to China with us for trial...."

"No."

Wang's eyes narrowed. "No? They rebel against your father. They rebel against the Dragon Throne. In time, perhaps soon, they will rebel against you."

Yi Xiao dismissed the suggestion with a negligent wave of his hand. "Oh, I sincerely doubt that. But we can discuss that question later, once these other men have been dealt with." He turned his attention on Jeffreys, adding, "Unless I'm seriously mistaken, you are the leader of these men?"

Jeffreys picked thoughtfully at his teeth with a delicate white splinter that put Zak in mind of bone. Silently, he looked Yi Xiao up and down before finally saying, "I see no one here worthy of my attention." His thick drawl was pure deep south and his arrogant sneer was pure plantation master. "Where is the white man who commands this camp?"

Zak realized Jeffreys didn't know Caleb had died. Or, perhaps, he'd thought the camp, like the valley he'd been trying to steal, belonged to Hal Kraft now? "I own this land, mister," he said quietly.

That resulted in a snort as cold as ice. "A black man pretends to own land? I think not. Where is the real owner?"

Now it was Jo's turn to talk and she took it. "I'm the only white person here, mister. And I own half this camp, so if you can't bear to put your words to my partner, you can be telling them to me."

The man's eyes seemed to glow from inside and it wasn't a reflection. Fire didn't have a sick yellow-green tint like corpse-lights. Zak moved forward to set himself between Jo and Jeffreys and found Yi Xiao doing the same.

Slowly Jeffreys recovered himself. "Where's your Pa, little girl. I'll do business with him if you don't mind."

"You can't. Pa died on the way here and I'm his only heir. So I say again, you tell me what you want or you go away."

Another flare, this one bright enough to send most of the miners, and Jeffreys' men, huddling backwards. Wang's men were soldiers and apparently had seen such things before. All they did was set themselves, prepared to dodge or attack as ordered. Zak stayed where he was as well, saying, "There's no point in getting angry, sir. We don't even know who you are, much less why you think you have business here."

Before Jeffreys could insult Zak again, Jo added, "You're the uninvited guest here. Ain't right for you to waltz in making trouble without so much as an introduction."

Stiff as a board, Jeffreys snapped, "I am Doctor Tyrone P. Jeffreys, late of Atlanta. That's all you need know." He bowed mockingly, adding, "Now then, little miss. I know your name's Jo, but I don't know the rest of it."

She was about to answer, but Zak realized in time what a mistake it'd be. "No. Don't say a thing," he said quickly. At the same time, Yi Xiao added, "He has a new tool to replace the one I destroyed. Don't give it a weapon against you."

As Jo fell silent Jeffreys turned blazing eyes on Yi Xiao. "You destroyed? You're an ignorant savage. What do you know of power and magic?"

"Master says, those who seek power over others should first master themselves." Yi Xiao's hands sparked as he raised them. "This ignorant savage has not yet achieved that goal, but he is more than a match for a dead thing forced to exist beyond its time."

Almost everyone, including Wang and his men, backed away. Not from Yi Xiao's power but from the bone chilling energy emanating from Jeffreys.

The man pointed at the fire with his cane and it suddenly went dark, so that the only light came from him. Zak grabbed Jo and dragged her back, knowing he couldn't help. The man's skeleton seemed to be burning from within, the same sickening corpse-fire that shone from his eyes.

Something fluttered in the air between Jeffreys and Yi Xiao. "I know your name," Jeffreys said calmly. "Lang Yi Xiao, the Wanderer. Least worthy and youngest son of the House of the White Wolf."

The thing's substance darkened as what little remained of Burns took shape. More shadows thickened into human shapes; some unfamiliar, others the men the Bone Marrow Eater had killed. All drew close, crying out in pain but forced by Jeffreys' will to act.

Yi Xiao smiled. "True," he agreed. "But I'm also the best and only disciple of the Storm Hermit." As he spoke a bolt of lightning rose from around his feet to pierce the sky above.

ooo

The energies flowing through Yi Xiao weren't just his *qi* this time. Close as he was to one of the roots of the world, he'd automatically and without thinking about it, reached deep. If he'd been closer to its source it would have burned him to a crisp. This far away it jolted through his body and shuddered through every nerve. He let it, balancing atop the power as if he was perched atop Heng Shan's highest peak.

"Lang Yi Xiao, the Wanderer. Least worthy and youngest son of the House of the White Wolf." The souls his enemy had stolen shrieked his name over and over, trying to worm their way into his thoughts. They could not. The force of the world raged through him, overwhelming all else.

No mortal could take such power for long and Yi Xiao was as mortal as any man. He knew he had to act quickly, before what was human in him was burned away. He spread his hands, centering himself, maintaining his position despite the energies trying to transform him.

It was the hardest thing he'd ever done. By nature he was active, a constantly moving force upon the world. Making himself the center of so much power, making himself its focus, was not his natural state at all. He corrected himself, remembering his teachings. "Master says, it is not the world that centers on you, but you upon the world."

Time slowed. Time stopped. He found himself hanging between seconds, face to face with the men Jeffreys had killed and bound. Their torment was obvious, for they were trapped in this timeless state, unable to die and unable to return to life. They sought other lives, hoping to find their way out of their bondage, but could not be free.

Or could they? "His name is Doctor Tyrone P. Jeffreys, late of Atlanta."

Time sped forward. Jeffreys' victims howled triumphantly. The earth shook. The wind wailed. The others cowered in terror. Only Jeffreys didn't move, too certain of his control to react. The paper-thin remnants of the lives he'd stolen and enslaved spun round him, a whirlwind of rage and desolation.

"Use my strength," Yi Xiao said, offering it freely. "Save yourselves."

By the time Jeffreys realized he was no longer their master it was too late. They tore the clothes from his flesh, his flesh from his bones and shattered his bones to dust. Until all that was left was a mewling yellow-green worm that somehow managed to dig into the dirt and escape, his victims following behind, howling.

Yi Xiao released his hold on the power he'd summoned, letting it sink back into the roots of the world. Standing in near darkness, all he could do was take deep, slow, breaths. Somehow, he stayed upright, though his knees and legs trembled from the effort.

Light flared as someone relit the fire. Others were babbling prayers, still others curses. Then someone said in Manchurian, "Commander, that thing called him...." The voice broke off suddenly, accompanied by a sound Yi Xiao knew only too well. He raised his head, tried to turn and crumpled to the ground, staring at Wang as the man drew his sword from his own soldier's throat.

"What... why are you...."

Wang ignored Yi Xiao's weak protests, gesturing to his lieutenants. "Kill them."

As the two men drew their swords, walking slowly towards their former compatriots, Yi Xiao struggled to stand. "Help them," he called to the miners. "Don't let them do this."

Once again Gan Han tossed Yi Xiao's sabre to his feet. "You stop them. They're your responsibility." Despite what she said, she drew her own weapon, blocking the pair from attacking their own cowering men.

Yi Xiao ignored his weapon where it lay. He didn't have the strength to fight, no matter how much he wanted to. "Wang! Stop your men. Now."

"They've heard the truth. All these men have heard the truth. They can't be allowed to live, your Highness. The Xianfeng Emperor—your twin— sits upon the Dragon Throne now, but when we bring you home we will make you Emperor in his stead."

Yi Xiao stared at the man. "You knew I wasn't Yi Zhu. Wait... Xianfeng Emperor? My twin?"

"Your father, your true father, died three months ago, your Highness. Despite my commander, General Hwei's best efforts, that hag Madam Lang snuck your brother into the Summer Palace just in time for him to be declared heir. Hwei sent me to find you, so you can take your brother's place unnoticed."

The very idea was laughable. Even more laughable than Wang believing he was Yi Zhu, gallivanting off to America while his father, the Emperor, died. "You're an idiot."

Wang's expression darkened. "What?"

"Were you listening just then? Did you hear those things call my name, my true name?"

"But...."

"But I was born in the Summer Palace, on the very same day as my cousin Yi Zhu. I know the rumors saying I'm his twin and a threat to his inheritance. Saying Madam Lang took me into her family to protect the lineage...."

"You are those things. You're the only one to save us from that fool on the throne's stupidities."

"No. The rumors are wrong. You're wrong. I'm not Yi Zhu's twin. I'm the youngest son of Lang Mianzhen, grandson of the Imperial Princess He Xiao. Great grandson of the Qianglong Emperor and of the traitor, Lang Heshen. My father is the Duke of Jin and my mother a Princess of Tu. And I will not be used as a pawn to give General Hwei a puppet on the throne."

Wang drew his sword. "I don't have to kill you to defeat you," he growled. "You can barely...." He didn't finish the sentence. He'd been so focused on Yi Xiao he hadn't noticed Zak moving slowly up behind him, iron staff in hand. The thump to the back of his head wasn't hard, but it was enough.

"That... was an unfair and effective solution," Yi Xiao told the man.

"Would you like me to wake him up so you can go back to fighting?"

"No. No, not really." Yi Xiao grinned wryly, his arms giving way now that they were no longer needed to prop him up. "In fact, I'd much prefer taking a nap for a while." Without bothering to wait for an answer he did just that.

○○○

When he woke the next day, Wang raved and cursed, fighting the ropes holding him down and frothing at the mouth like a madman. His men, having realized he and his two lieutenants were traitors, ignored his demands to be freed, willingly assisting the miners in their work.

As for Jeffreys' men; without the sorcerer and his terrible magic to keep them in line, most drifted off. Some remained, hiring on with the Chinese miners in the hopes of earning enough to buy a share along with the others. Jeffreys' sabotage had turned out serendipitous, for it'd revealed a vein of gold in the rock that Ma and his men might have missed otherwise. It might not be enough to make them rich, but it was a start.

Zak spent most of his spare time working on a special project for Yi Xiao, one the young man insisted he keep secret from everyone. Jo practiced the exercises Yi Xiao had taught her and helped keep the camp running. Her arguments with Chao often resulted in chases that had those watching laying bets as to who would win the latest fight. Zak could tell from the way both children laughed that it was just a game. One that might turn to something else, if he read their characters rightly.

Aside from overseeing Zak's work, Yi Xiao spent a great deal of his time just sitting in one place, completely ignoring the chaos around him, including Gan Han's continuous attempts to get him to draw his blade. Zak had a feeling it'd take some truly remarkable circumstances to force Yi Xiao into action but he didn't bother trying to persuade the young lady. He could tell she wouldn't listen.

At last, almost a full week after Jeffrey's final attack on the camp, Yi Xiao looked up from his meditations to say. "I believe it's time for me to go."

"Where are we going?" Gan Han demanded. "Your grandmother may have sent you to America, but that doesn't mean you have to wander all over the place."

Zak wasn't surprised at Yi Xiao's bland answer. "Second question first. She also didn't say I had to stay in one place. I don't have to wander. I want to." He rose to his feet, fending off the girl's attack with ease. "First question last. You're not coming with me."

"Nonsense. I will follow you wherever you go until we duel."

The girl's response was no more surprising than Yi Xiao's. Yet Zak couldn't help asking, "What did he do to you to make you so determined to fight him?"

It was Yi Xiao who explained, "Her family demands it of her. Her family is mad. If I were still the person I was before I joined the Wind and

Rain sect, I'd probably have killed her." At Zak's shocked stare, he added, "She's not my match. She knows it, yet still tries to fight me. No one in the martial world would blame me at all if I stabbed her to the heart."

"But she's a girl...."

"The rules of the martial world are harsh, Zak. Gan Han knows it." The girl inclined her head gravely, agreeing, and Yi Xiao continued, "Women can and do take high positions within it, but they cannot expect to be exempt from the danger simply because they're women. Not and retain the right to take those positions."

The very idea disgusted and shook Zak to his core. He'd seen Yi Xiao at his most ferocious and the thought of him cutting pretty little Gan Han down was terrifying. "Is that why you left the martial world, then?"

"Part of it." Yi Xiao's expression went distant. "I killed my first man when I was fourteen. To be fair, he was trying to kill me, so I didn't really have a choice. But I liked it. I wanted to do it again. Yet at the same time it sickened me. I didn't want to be the person I was becoming. I sought out the most dangerous, most difficult to persuade, teacher. If she killed me, I'd be done with the killing. If she accepted me, I'd learn to master my violence. I haven't, yet, but I've learned to harness it."

Gan Han looked away and Zak guessed she didn't want to admit she was asking too much of the man. "Then all you have to do is fight me and I will prove my skill against yours, as I was commanded."

"You are not my match. We both know it."

"I do not know anything of the sort." Gan Han's voice trembled and Zak knew she was lying.

"I could prove it, here and now, but I will make a deal with you instead." Yi Xiao pointed to Wang's men. "Take them, and the traitors, to my grandmother in China. Tell her what Wang and Hwei meant to do and give her this letter." He took an envelope from his shirt pocket and held it out.

"And you'll come home to fight me?"

"I won't come home until grandmother sends for me. But you may return to America, if that's still your wish."

"And then you'll fight me."

"Again, no." Before Gan Han could argue more, Yi Xiao added, "When you find me, given you can, I will teach you my blade techniques. I will make you at least the weapons master I was before I became the Storm Hermit's disciple. You may even become my better. That's what your family wants, after all, for you to take my place in the ranks of the martial world."

Gan Han hesitated. Took the envelope. "I will find you. I have your sabre and it will call to you."

Zak almost opened his mouth to protest, then realized what Yi Xiao was doing in time. Only when Gan Han had gone off to gather her things and talk to Wang's men did he say, "That's why you had me copy your weapon."

"It was."

"You switched it."

"I did."

"So even if she could use your sabre to find you, she won't have it."

"That's right." Yi Xiao smiled wryly. "She's a stubborn child. I'm sure she'll still try to find me. She may even succeed. But I don't see any reason to make it easier for her."

Zak chuckled. "So you're leaving now? Before she notices?"

"Of course." Yi Xiao bowed. "I appreciate you letting me stay in camp for as long as I have. But I'm not called The Wanderer for nothing and it's time for me to live up to my name."

As the young man disappeared into the trees, as slippery and impossible to hold onto as ever, Zak reflected that he had more than enough adventure ahead of him, given the way things were in California right then.

Of course, that was probably exactly the way Yi Xiao wanted it.

Epilogue —
Advancing to one's Potential

TO: The Imperial Princess Qing He Xiao. Last daughter of the beloved Emperor Qianlong. Head of the White Wolf Clan
FROM: The wandering priest Yi Xiao. Second son of Lang Mingzhen, the Duke of Jin and Lady Tu, Princess of Tu in Khaitan

Beloved Grandmother,

I stand atop Mount Tam and clasp my hands to the center of the world.

When last we met, you commanded I travel to the American territory of California. At the time, I believed you meant me to act as decoy while my cousin Yi Zhu escaped to meet his father, the honored and honorable Daoguang Emperor. Indeed, I am sure that was your primary purpose at the time.

Yet circumstances here in America, a chance meeting with General Hwei's cohort, Commander Wang, has revealed a deeper purpose to my exile. And exile it must be. As long as my illustrious—and now Imperial—cousin sits upon the Dragon throne I, as his apparent twin, shall always be a threat to him. He may or may not realize it, but others will, and will seek to use me. Just as Commander Wang intended to.

The young lady who brings you this message will tell you how I came to meet with this Commander Wang and the full nature of the treachery he planned. Aside from his two lieutenants, Huan and Fu, his men are innocent. He would have killed them when they learned I was not who Wang pretended I was. Please see to it they are fairly treated. They could not know his intentions.

Regarding the young lady.... She is Gan Han, a daughter of the Xihua clan and their finest swords-master. She was ordered to seek me out in battle, even brought my sabre to me from where I left it on Heng Shan. I'm sure she believes her purpose was to raise her position in the martial world, since defeating my blade—at the risk of arrogance—is no easy thing.

I also suspect, or fear, an ulterior purpose, one I cannot help but decry. Neither she, nor I, are breeding stock nor tools of political maneuvering. You, yourself, taught me that. Yet her family likely believe that I will become attracted to a woman of her skill and inevitably fall in love. Be kind to her. Protect her, if you will, from their machinations. I do not love her, nor do I think I ever will, but she has been a comrade in arms and I would not have her mistreated.

I have learned much and have much more to learn. Yet I miss and love you all. Give my love to all the family. Tell them that my body may walk these strange lands until the end of my days, but my heart will walk with all of you for eternity.

I shall clasp my hands to the center of the world.

Be safe. Be well. May our people prosper, our crops grow fertile and the train I know my father would have us build fly on its rails with great speed and greater safety. May your years be long and may we meet again.

With love and profound respect,
Lang Yi Xiao
Priest and Wanderer.

THE END

ABOUT OUR CREATORS

AUTHOR –

BARBARA DORAN—has been making up stories for as long as she can remember. From playing Ms. Marvel to her best friend's Captain Marvel to writing new stories for old characters (Hannibal King, X-Men, Green Hornet, The Saint, The Shadow and many others), to writing gaming and anime fanfiction online.

After ten years behind the keyboard as a software engineer, Barbara realized that her true love wasn't coding but making stuff up. So when she left that career in favor of dealing with two frequent interruptions of her life (namely her own personal Tiger and Dragon), she decided to use what little time they allowed her to work on writing. Her Long Suffering Husband, without whom she could never have managed such a goal, has been nothing if not supportive.

Along with reading every mystery, SF and fantasy book she could get her hands on, Barbara grew up watching Star Trek, Batman, Green Hornet, along with the usual Saturday morning cartoons. She became addicted to shows like Battle of the Planets and Doctor Who in her teens and discovered Run Run Shaw's martial arts flicks some years later. Those influences, along with a love of folklore and mythology, have become part of the world some small portion of her mind lives in. When, of course, she isn't chasing Tiger and Dragon from one school event to another.

Barbara can be contacted at <BarbaraDoran@sumergoscriptum.com>. Her website is <http://www.sumergoscriptum.com/barbaradoran/>.

INTERIOR ILLUSTRATOR –

GARY KATO – was born in Honolulu, in 1949. He graduated from the University of Hawaii with a Bachelor in Fine Arts degree. His comic book work has appeared in such varied titles as Destroyer Duck, Thunderbunny, Ms. Tree and Mr. Jigsaw. He's also illustrated children's books such as The Menehune of Naupaka Village and the currently available Barry Baskerville Returns and Jamie and the Fish-Eyed Goggles. He's also been a contributor to the Children's Television Workshop magazines, 3-2-1 Contact and Kid City.

COVER ARTIST–

ROB DAVIS—began his professional art career doing illustrations for role-playing games in the late 1980's. Not long after he began lettering and inking, then penciling comics for a number of small black and white comics publishers- most notably for Eternity Comics, which eventually became Malibu Comics in the 1990's, on their book SCIMIDAR with writer R.A. Jones. Branching out to other black and white publishers and eventually working at both DC and Marvel Rob worked on likeness intensive comics like TV adaptations of QUANTUM LEAP and STAR TREK's many incarnations mostly on the DEEP SPACE NINE comics for Malibu. At Marvel he worked on the Saturday morning cartoon adaptation PIRATES OF DARK WATER. After the comics industry implosion in the late 1990's Rob picked up work on video games, advertising illustration and T-shirt design as well as some small press comics like ROBYN OF SHERWOOD for Caliber. Rob continues to do the occasional self-published comic book as well as publisher and designer for his small-press production REDBUD STUDIO COMICS. Rob is Art Director, Designer and Illustrator for the New Pulp production outfit AIRSHIP 27 partnered with writer/editor Ron Fortier. Rob is the recipient of the PULP FACTORY AWARD for "Best Interior Illustrations" in 2010 and 2016 for his work on SHERLOCK HOLMES: CONSULTING DETECTIVE and has been nominated for the same award every year since the its inception. He works and lives in central Missouri with his wife and two children.

From the same author:

TROUBLE IN STRIKERSPORT

When a mysterious evil force known only as the Voice begins to take control of the local mobs in the coast city of Strikersport, two new heroes appear on the scene. Their origin, the neighborhood streets of Chinatown. The masked Tiger and Dragon wield both science and magic in their battle to combat the forces of darkness. Soon several of the city's prominent citizens become players in this cataclysmic war. These include players from a wealthy family with roots to Strikersport history, a rookie cop and a crusading newspaper editor.

Writer Barbara Doran spins a classic pulp adventure with breakneck pacing, original characters and a tangled plot that will keep readers guessing to the very end. Mixing martial arts with Chinese mysticism, she offers a truly unique action mystery sure to entertain readers from beginning to end.

MYSTERIES OF SHANGHAI

Shanghai in the 1930s is a place of excitement and intrigue... and magic. It is an international hotspot where foreign agents from around the world ply their trade. Brought to Shanghai to investigate a powerful new aircraft engine, young Conall McLeod becomes embroiled in a high-stakes game between gangs, spies and immortal beings. Together with his beloved Mudan Chang and hot-shot Chinese pilot, Feng Zhanchi, Conall must navigate the dangerous waters of the city's criminal undercurrents and help free a lost immortal from the clutches of evil.

Writer Barbara Doran spins a fantastic tale of action and mystery filled with some of the most memorable characters ever conceived. Whether deep within the city's maze of dark alleys or high atop an ancient castle of evil, none will be able to escape from The Wings of the Golden Dragon!

HAVOK IN STRIKERSPORT

As the Feast of Hungry Ghosts begins in the northwest port city of Strikersport, monsters and actual ghosts begin appearing throughout the city causing all manner of chaos. Thus the city's twin protectors, Dragon and Tiger, enter the fray and set about uncovering the reason behind the sudden appearances.

Their revelations lead back in time to a horrendous massacre in the village of Batsu, a province of the magical kingdom of Khaitan. Have agents of ancient deities come to Strikersports to wreak vengeances on the guilty? And if so, what is the magical artifact and its connection to an animated shi shi lion roaming free through the city?

PULP FICTION FOR A NEW GENERATION!

AN AIRSHIP 27 PRODUCTION
AIRSHIP27HANGAR.COM

FOR AVAILABILITY: AIRSHIP27HANGAR.COM

Coming Soon from Airship 27 Productions:

VOLUME 12

Sherlock Holmes
Consulting Detective

THE NOTTINGHAM CRAKSTER
&
THE HANGMAN'S DAUGHTER
By I.A. Watson

THE COUNTERFEIT SECRETARY
By Barbara Doran

THE PEPPERBOX AFFAIR
By Fred Adams Jr.

THE ADVENTURE OF THE
STOLEN TATTOO
By Brad Mengel

Printed in Great Britain
by Amazon

77291385R00088